if she ran

(a kate wise mystery—book 3)

blake pierce

CHAPTER ONE

Her nerves were on fire and she felt like she might get sick at any moment. The boxing gloves on her hands felt foreign and the head gear was suffocating. Neither of these things were new to Kate Wise—she had been training for about two months now, but this was her first time sparring with an actual partner. While she was aware that it was all in good fun and just part of the workout regimen, it was still making her nervous. She'd be throwing actual punches at someone's body and that was not something she had ever taken lightly.

She looked across the ring at her sparring partner, a younger woman whom she was trying her best not to view as an *opponent*. She was another member of the small gym who had been undergoing the boxing program. The woman's name was Margo Dunn and she was taking the course for the same reason as Kate; it was a great full body exercise that, at its core, didn't involve too much running or weightlifting.

Margo grinned at Kate as her trainer slipped in her mouth guard. Kate nodded back in response as her trainer slid hers in as well. When it fell in perfectly around her teeth, Kate felt as if a switch had been flipped. She was in boxing mode now. Yes, the nerves were still there and she was uneasy with the whole situation, but it was time to go. It was time to work. There was only an audience of seven—made up of trainers and two other gym members who were just curious.

By the side of the ring, someone rang the little bell to signify the start of the fight. Kate walked out to the middle of the ring, where she met with Margo. They tapped gloves and took two respectful steps back.

And then it was on. Kate circled a bit, finding the rhythm with her feet she had been taught to remember as if she were dancing. She stepped forward and threw her first jab. Margo blocked it easily, but it was good to just get warmed up. Kate jabbed again, a little rabbit punch with her left hand. Margo blocked this one and then countered with a left that caught Kate right along the side of the head. The punch was soft by design—this was, after all, just a sparring match—and fell right along the cushion of the head gear. But still, it was enough to rock Kate a bit.

1

You're fifty-six, she thought to herself. *What the hell were you thinking?*

She considered the question as Margo threw a right-handed hook. Kate sidestepped it. Dodging it so easily gave her more confidence. When she also managed to effortlessly block the jab Margo followed with, it stirred up the need to excel.

You know why you're doing this, she thought. *Nine weeks in and you've lost eighteen pounds and have the best muscle tone you've had in your life. You feel about twenty years younger and let's be real...have you ever felt this strong?*

No, she hadn't. And while she was nowhere near mastering the art of boxing, she knew that she had the basic skills down.

With this mentality locked in place, she stepped forward in a near-strafing position, faked a left jab, and then delivered a right hook. When the hook landed right along Margo's chin, Kate sent out the left jab...and then another. Both landed true, rocking Margo a bit. A light of surprise shone in her eyes as she staggered back against the ropes. She grinned, though. Like Kate, she knew this was more or less just practice and she had just learned a lesson: be on the lookout for hard fakes at all times.

Margo responded with two jabs to the body, one that connected with Kate's ribs. The wind went rushing out of her for a moment and by the time she had caught it again, she saw the heavy right hook coming from her left. She tried moving but hadn't caught it in time. It slammed into the side of her padded head and shook her backward.

She was dizzy for a moment. Her vision blurred and her knees felt a little weak. She thought about falling, just to catch a break.

Yeah...too old for this.

But then the counter to that was: *You know any other women over fifty who could take this punch and remain standing?*

Kate responded with two jabs and then a blow to the body. Only one of the jabs landed but the body blow struck its target. Margo went back into the ropes, staggering a bit. She then came back off of the ropes and threw an impatient uppercut. It was not designed to land. It was just meant to cause Kate to bring her arms up to block it so Margo could then deliver jabs to her exposed core. But Kate saw the slight hesitation in the delivery, knowing the purpose behind it. Instead of blocking the punch, she stepped hard to the right, waited for the full delivery to swing through, and then threw a hard right-handed jab that connected with the side of Margo's head.

2

Margo went down right away. She fell on her stomach and rolled over quickly. She slid back to her corner and popped out her mouth guard. She smiled at Kate and shook her head in disbelief.

"I'm sorry," Kate said, kneeling down in front of Margo.

"Don't be," Margo said. "It honestly makes no sense how you manage to be that fast. I feel like I need to apologize. Because of your age, I assumed you'd be...slower."

Kate's trainer—a grizzled sixty-something man with a long white beard—climbed between the ropes, chuckling. "I made that same mistake," he said. "Had a black eye for about a week because of it. Caught the exact same punch that just knocked you down."

"Don't feel so apologetic," Kate said. "That one to my head was huge. It almost got me."

"It *should* have gotten you," the trainer said. "Honestly, it was a little harder than I like to see in these simple sparring matches." He then looked to Margo. "Up to you. You want to keep going?"

Margo nodded and pulled herself up. Again, her trainer put her mouthpiece in. Both women returned to their respective corners and waited for the bell.

But it was not the bell that Kate heard. Instead, she heard the ringing of her phone. And it was the assigned ringer she used for all calls that came from the bureau.

She pushed her mouthpiece out of her mouth and held her gloved hands out to her trainer. "Sorry," she said. "I have to take that."

Her trainer knew about her part-time job as a special agent. He thought it was hard-ass (his word, not hers) that she refused to entirely retire from such a job. So when he untied her gloves for her, he did so as quickly as possible.

Kate slid between the ropes and ran to her gym bag, which was sitting by the wall. She always kept it out and not in the locker room just in case she got such a call. She grabbed the phone and her heart surged with excitement and despair all at once when she saw Deputy Director Duran's name on the display.

"This is Agent Wise," she said.

"Wise, it's Duran. You got a second?"

"I do," she said, glancing back at the ring with longing. Margo's trainer was working with her on how to avoid fake-outs. "What can I do for you?"

"I was hoping you could come in on a case. It's effective immediately, and I'd need you and DeMarco to fly out tonight."

"I don't know," she said. And that was the truth. It was very sudden and she had spoken to Melissa, her daughter, several times

3

in the last few weeks about not being so readily available for the last-minute jobs. She had been spending much more time with Melissa and Michelle, her granddaughter, over the last month or so and they finally had a good thing going—something like a routine. Something like a family.

"I appreciate you thinking of me," Kate said. "But I don't know if I can come in for this one. It's very last minute. And flying out…that makes it seem like it's pretty far away. I don't know that I'm prepared for a long trip. Where is it, anyway?"

"New York. Kate…I'm pretty sure it has ties to the Nobilini case."

The name sent a chill through her. Her head started ringing, and it wasn't from the blow Margo had delivered moments ago. Flashes of a case from nearly eight years ago cascaded through her head—leering, taunting.

"Kate?"

"I'm here," she said. She then looked back to the ring. Margo was stretching and lightly jogging in place, ready for their next bout.

It was a shame she wouldn't get it. Because as soon as Kate heard the name, she knew she'd take the case. She had to.

The Nobilini case had gotten away from her eight years ago—one of the true defeats she'd ever had in her career.

This was her chance to close it—to bolt shut the one case that had truly bested her.

"When's the flight?" she asked Duran.

"Dulles to JFK, leaves in four hours."

She thought of Melissa and Michelle, her heart sinking. Melissa wouldn't understand, but Kate could not turn this opportunity down.

"I'll be on it," she said.

CHAPTER TWO

Kate managed to pack and make it out of Richmond in less than an hour and a half. When she met her partner, Kristen DeMarco, outside of one of the many Starbucks in Dulles International Airport, they had only ten minutes remaining before takeoff; most of the plane's passengers had already boarded.

As DeMarco started power-walking toward Kate with her coffee in hand, she smiled and shook her head. "If you'd just go ahead and move to DC, you wouldn't be rushing and borderline late all the time."

"No can do," Kate said as they joined together and starting hurrying for the gate. "It's enough that this so-called part-time job is keeping me away from my family more than I'd like. If it was a requirement that I live in DC, I wouldn't be doing it at all."

"How *are* Melissa and little Michelle?" DeMarco asked.

"They're doing well. I spoke with Melissa on my way here. She said she understood and wished me luck. And for the first time, I think she actually meant it."

"Good. I told you she'd come around. I assume it would be cool as hell to have a bad-ass for a mother."

"I'm far from a bad-ass," Kate said as they reached the gate. Still, she thought of what she had been doing when she received the call and thought it might be okay to accept that moniker...at least a little.

"Last I heard," Kate said, "you were working a triple murder case out in Maine."

"Yeah, I was. We wrapped it about a week ago—about six agents in all on that thing. When I got the call from Duran about this case, he told me he planned to send you out and asked if I wanted to partner with you. I, of course, jumped at the chance. I told him I'd like to be partnered with you whenever possible in the future."

"Thanks," Kate said. She left it at that, though. It actually meant a lot to her but she didn't want to get sappy on DeMarco.

They boarded the plane together and took their seats, right beside one another. When they were settled, DeMarco reached into her carry-on and pulled out a thick folder crammed with papers and documents.

"This is everything on the Nobilini file," she said. "Based on your history with it, I assume you know it inside and out?"

"Probably," Kate said.

"It's a pretty quick flight," DeMarco pointed out. "I'd much rather hear it from you instead of notes and files."

Kate would have felt the same way. What surprised her was how eager she was to share the details of the case with DeMarco. The case had been like a nagging itch at the back of her mind over the years but she had always managed to push it away, not wanting to focus on the one true failure of her career.

So as the plane started to position itself toward the runway, Kate started to go back over the specifics of the case. As she did, stopping for the annoyance of the pre-flight announcements, she realized that it all felt new now. Maybe it was all the time that had passed since she had last truly dwelt on it, or the almost-retirement (or both), but the case now felt alive and active.

She told DeMarco the details of the case in a high-end suburb just out of New York City. Just one body, but the case had been pushed by someone in Congress, as the victim was closely linked. No prints, no clues. The body, one Frank Nobilini, was found in an alley in the Midtown district. The best guess was that he had been headed for work, walking the single block from the parking garage to his office. Just a single gunshot wound to the back of the head. Execution style.

"How could it be execution style if someone clearly abducted him and dragged him into the alleyway?" DeMarco asked.

"That's another unanswered question to the case. It was assumed that Nobilini was roughed up a bit, forced to his knees, and then shot in the back of the head. Blood and bits of skull were all over the side of the wall of the building beside the body. His BMW keys were still in his hand."

DeMarco nodded and allowed Kate to continue.

"The victim was from a small town, a well-to-do little suburb called Ashton," Kate said. "It's the sort of town that draws in visitors for its pretentious antique stores, overpriced dining, and immaculate real estate."

"And that's the thing I don't get about it," DeMarco said. "A place like that, people tend to gossip, right? You'd think *someone* would have known something or heard rumors about who the killer was. But there's nothing in these files." She said this last bit as she thumped her fingers against the folder.

"That always unnerved me," Kate said. "Ashton is an upscale place. But outside of that, it's also a very tight community.

Everyone knows each other. For the most part, everyone was polite to one another. Neighbors helping neighbors, big turn-outs for school bake sales, the whole nine yards. The place is squeaky clean."

"No motives for the killer?" DeMarco asked.

"None that I ever knew about. Ashton has a population of just over three thousand. And sure, while it does attract its fair amount of people from New York City and other outlying areas, it has an incredibly small crime rate. So even though the murder didn't actually occur in Ashton, it's why the Nobilini murder was such a big deal eight years ago."

"And there were never any other murders like this one?"

"Nope. Not until today, apparently. My theory is that the killer noted the FBI presence and got spooked. In a town that size, it would be easy to notice the presence of the FBI." Kate paused here and took the file folder from DeMarco. "How much did Duran tell you?"

"Not much. He said we were in a rush and asked that I read over the case files."

"Did you see what sort of gun was used for the murder?" Kate asked.

"I did. A Ruger Hunter Mark IV. Seemed weird. Seemed *professional*. That's an expensive gun for some random murder with no apparent motive."

"I agree. The bullet and the casing we found made it an easy one to recognize. And despite the expensive and very nice gun that was used, the fact that it was used at all told us all we needed to know: it was someone that knew jack shit about killing people."

"How's that?"

"Anyone that knew what they were doing would know that the Ruger Hunter Mark IV would leave behind a casing. Which makes it a terrible choice."

"I assume this latest man was killed by a similar weapon?" DeMarco asked.

"According to Duran, it's the exact same weapon."

"So this killer decided to do it again eight years later. Weird."

"Well, we'll have to wait and see about that," Kate said. "All Duran told me was that the victim looked as if he had been set up like a prop. And that the weapon used to kill him was the same kind that killed Frank Nobilini."

"Yeah, and this one is in Midtown in New York City. I wonder if this latest victim is also connected to Ashton."

Kate only shrugged as the plane experienced a bit of turbulence. It had done her a great deal of good to go through the case details. It had essentially knocked the cobwebs off of the case and made it feel new again. And maybe, Kate figured, eight years of space between her and the original case might allow her to look at it with fresh eyes.

***

It had been a while since Kate had been to New York. She and Michael, her late husband, had come here for a weekend getaway not long before he died. The congestion and absolute busyness of the place never ceased to awe her. It made the gridlock of Washington, DC, seem trivial by comparison. The fact that it was nearing nine o'clock on a Friday night was not helping matters.

They arrived at the scene of the crime at 8:42 p.m. Kate parked their rental car as close to the crime scene tape as she could. The scene was in a back alley located on 43rd Street, the hustle and bustle of Grand Central Station a few blocks over. There were two police cars parked nose to nose in front of the alley, not blocking the yellow crime scene tape or the alley itself, but making it known to anyone who wanted a peek at what was going on that there would be repercussions for their curiosity.

As Kate and DeMarco reached the alleyway, a bulky policeman stopped them at the crime scene tape. But when Kate showed her badge, he shrugged his shoulders and lifted the tape for them. She noted that he made no real attempt to check out DeMarco when she bent down to go under the tape. She wondered idly if DeMarco, an openly homosexual woman, took offense when a man checked her out or if she considered it a compliment.

"Feds," the officer said with a huff. "I heard they called you in. Seems a bit much to me. Pretty open and shut case from the looks of it."

"Just checking on something," Kate said as she and DeMarco walked into the dark alley.

The police cars at the mouth of the alley had been parked at a light angle to allow the headlights to shine into the darkness. Kate's and DeMarco's elongated shadows added an air of eeriness to the scene.

At the back of the alleyway—which dead-ended along a brick wall—there were two policemen and a plainclothes detective standing in a small semicircle. There was a slight lump against the wall in front of them. The victim, Kate presumed. She approached

8

the three men and introduced herself and DeMarco as they again showed their ID.

"Nice to meet you," one of the officers said. "But if I'm being honest, I don't quite know why the FBI was so insistent on getting someone out here."

"Ah, Jesus," the plainclothes detective said. He looked to be in his forties and a bit grungy. Long dark hair, five o'clock shadow, and a pair of glasses that reminded Kate of every picture she'd ever seen of Buddy Holly.

"We've been through this," the detective said. He looked at Kate, rolled his eyes, and said: "If it's a crime that's older than a week or so, NYPD doesn't want to touch it. It blows their minds that anyone would want to dig back up an unsolved murder case from eight years ago. I was actually the one that called the bureau. I know they were hot and heavy on the Nobilini case when it was active. Some sort of friendship with someone in Congress, right?"

"That's right," Kate said. "And I was the lead agent on that case."

"Oh. Good to meet you. I'm Detective Luke Pritchard. I sort of have an obsession with cold cases. This one pinged my interest because of the weapon that seems to have been used as well as the fact that it was carried out execution style. If you look closely, you can see scuff marks on the forehead where the killer apparently had him lean against the brick wall right here." He placed his hand on the side of the building to their right where there was dried blood splattered everywhere.

"May we?" Kate asked.

The two policemen shrugged and stepped back. "By all means," one said. "With a detective and the bureau on this, we'll happily leave you to it."

"Have fun," the other cop said as they turned away and headed back to the mouth of the alleyway.

Kate and DeMarco crowded in around the body. Pritchard stepped back to allow them some extra room, but kept close.

"Well," DeMarco said, "I'd say the immediate cause of death is pretty clear."

This was true. There was a single bullet hole in the back of the man's head, the hole rather clean but the rim of it charred and gory—just like Frank Nobilini's. It was a man, in his late thirties or early forties if Kate had to venture a guess. He was wearing high-end athletic wear, a thin zip-up hoodie, and nice jogging pants. The laces of his expensive running shoes were tied perfectly and the

Apple ear buds he had been listening to sat neatly to his side, as if placed there intentionally.

"We have an ID yet?" Kate asked.

"Yeah," Pritchard said. "Jack Tucker. The ID in his wallet places his residence in the town of Ashton. Which, to me, was an even stronger connection to the Nobilini case."

"Are you familiar with Ashton, Detective?" Kate asked.

"Not very. Been through there a few times, but it's not my kind of place. Too perfect, too quaint and sickeningly sweet."

She knew what he meant. She couldn't help but wonder what he was going to feel like, having to return to Ashton.

"When was the body discovered?" DeMarco asked.

"Four thirty this afternoon. I arrived on the scene at a quarter after five and made all those connections. I had to beg them not to move the body until you guys got here. I figure you'd need to see the scene, body and all."

"I bet that made you popular," Kate commented.

"Oh, I'm used to it. I wish I was joking when I tell you that a lot of the cops around here call me Cold Case Pritchard."

"Well, I think on this one, you made the right call," Kate said. "Even if it turns out not to be connected, there's still someone out there that shot this man—someone that we need to find just in case this isn't an isolated incident."

"Yeah, no clue on my end," Pritchard said. "I have a few voice memos with my observations if you'd like to check them out."

"That could be helpful. I assume forensics has already snapped pictures?"

"Yeah. The digitals are probably already available."

With that, Kate got to her feet, her eyes still on Jack Tucker's body. His head was tilted to the right, as if he were staring longingly at the earbuds that had been so carefully placed by his side.

"Has the family been notified?" DeMarco asked.

"No. And I fear that because I asked the PD to hold off on moving the body and getting the case moved along, they're going to task me with it."

"If it's all the same, I'd prefer to do it," Kate said. "The fewer channels the details are being processed through, the better."

"If that's what you want."

Kate finally looked away from the body of Jack Tucker and then to the mouth of the alley where the two cops were congregating with the cop who had lifted the tape. She had delivered such devastating news more times than she cared to count and it was never easy. In fact, somehow, it seemed to get harder and harder.

But she had also learned that strangely enough, it was in the sharp and agonizing throes of grief that those suffering loss seemed to be able to remember the most minute of details.

Kate hoped it would hold true in this case.

And if so, maybe an unsuspecting new widow could help her close a case that had haunted her for nearly a decade.

CHAPTER THREE

It was only a twenty-minute drive from midtown to Ashton. It was 9:20 when they left the crime scene and the Friday night traffic remained stubborn and grueling. As they came out of the worst of the traffic and onto the freeway, Kate noticed that DeMarco was unusually quiet. She was in the passenger's seat, staring almost defiantly out the window at the passing cityscape.

"You okay over there?" Kate asked.

Without turning toward Kate, DeMarco answered right away, making it clear that something had been on her mind since leaving the crime scene.

"I know you've been at this awhile and know the ropes, but I've only ever had to break the news of a dead family member one time before. I hated it. It made me feel awful. And I really wish you had checked with me before volunteering us for it."

"I'm sorry. I didn't even think about that. But it *is* part of the job in some cases. At the risk of sounding cold, it's best to start getting used to it right off the bat. Besides...if we're running the case, what's the point in delegating this miserable task to that poor detective?"

"Still...how about a little heads-up on things like that in the future?"

The tone in her voice was one of anger, something she had not heard from DeMarco before—not directed toward her, anyway. "Yeah," she said, and left it at that.

They drove the rest of the way into Ashton in silence. Kate had worked enough cases where she had to break the news of a death to know that any tension between partners was going to make the matter so much worse. But she also knew that DeMarco wasn't the type who was going to listen to any lessons she had to deliver while she was pissed off. So maybe this one, Kate thought, would be something she could simply learn by living it out.

They arrived at the Tucker residence at 9:42. Kate was not at all surprised to see that the porch light, as well as just about every other light in the house, was on. From the looks of Jack Tucker's attire, he had been out for a morning jog. The question of why his body had been in the city, though, presented many questions. All of those questions presumably led to one very concerned wife.

A concerned wife who is about to find out she's now a widow, Kate thought. *My God, I hope they don't have kids.*

Kate parked in front of the house and got out of the car. DeMarco followed suit, only slower, as if to make sure to let Kate know that she was not at all happy about this particular detail. They walked up the flagstone walk toward the steps and Kate watched as the front door opened before they even made it to the porch.

The woman at the door saw them and froze. It looked as if she were working very hard to come up with what words she wanted to speak. In the end, all she could muster was: "Who are you?"

Kate slowly reached into her jacket pocket for her ID. Before she could even fully show it or give her name, the wife already knew. It showed in her eyes and the way her face slowly started to crumple. And as Kate and DeMarco finally reached the porch steps, Jack Tucker's wife went to her knees in the doorway and began to wail.

***

As it turned out, the Tuckers *did* have kids. Three of them, in fact, ages seven, ten, and thirteen. They were all still awake, lingering in the living room while Kate did her best to get the wife—Missy, she managed to introduce herself through her wailing and sobs—inside and sitting down. The thirteen-year-old came rushing to her mother's side while DeMarco did her best to keep the others away while their mother came to terms with the devastating news that she had just been handed.

In a way, Kate realized that maybe she *had* jumped the gun on DeMarco. The first twenty minutes she spent in the Tucker home that night were gut-wrenching. She could only think of one other moment in her career that was as heartbreaking. She looked over at DeMarco, both during and after she had tried to corral the kids, and saw the defiance and anger there. Kate figured this might be something that DeMarco held against her for a very long time.

Somewhere in the midst of it all, Missy Tucker realized that she was going to have to find someone to sit with her kids if she was going to try to be of any help to Kate and DeMarco. Through thin wails, she called her brother-in-law, having to break the news to him as well. They also lived in Ashton and his wife left almost immediately to come sit with the kids.

In an effort to give Missy and the Tucker children some privacy to deal with their grief, Kate got Missy's permission to look around the house for any signs of what might have occurred to have

13

resulted in someone wanting to murder her husband. They started in the master bedroom, searching through the Tuckers' bedside tables and private items to the sound of a sobbing family downstairs.

"This really sucks," DeMarco said.

"It does. I'm sorry, DeMarco. I really am. I just thought it would be easier for everyone involved."

"Is that really what it is?" DeMarco asked. "I know I don't know you all that well yet, but one of the things I *do* know about you is you have a tendency to go out of your way to put as much pressure on yourself as you can. It's why you can't figure out the rather simple struggle of balancing your time with the bureau with the time for your family."

"Excuse me?" Kate asked, feeling a flare of anger.

DeMarco shrugged. "Sorry. But it's true. Local cops could have done this and we could have probably already been elsewhere, digging into this case."

"With no witnesses, the wife is the best bet," Kate said. "It just so happens she's also having to deal with the death of her husband. It sucks for everyone involved. But you have to get over your own discomfort. In the grand scheme of things, who is more uncomfortable right now? You or the freshly grieving widow downstairs?"

Kate wasn't aware of her loud and irritated tone until the last few words were out of her mouth. DeMarco stared her down for a moment before shaking her head like some spoiled teenager with no rebuttal, and left the room.

When Kate also left the room, she saw that DeMarco was looking through an office and miniature library just down the hallway. Kate left her to it, opting to head outside to look for any clues. She wasn't expecting to find anything as she skirted around the house but knew it would be irresponsible not to go through the routine.

Back inside, she saw that Jack Tucker's brother and wife had come. The brother and Missy were in a trembling embrace while the wife knelt by the kids and gave them all a hug. Kate saw that the thirteen-year-old—a girl who looked very much like her father—had a blank look on her face. Seeing it, she didn't fault DeMarco for being pissed at her.

"Agent Wise?"

Kate turned as she was about to head back up the stairs and saw Missy coming down the hallway toward her. "Yes?"

"If we're going to talk, let's do it now. I don't know how much longer I can hold it together." Already, she was starting to let out little whines and moans again. Being that the news of her husband's death was barely one hour old, Kate admired her for her strength.

Missy said nothing else, but walked up the stairs with a quick glance back toward the living room where her kids and relatives were gathered. DeMarco joined them from where she was checking the medicine cabinet in the upstairs bathroom and the three of them went into the master bedroom—the bedroom Kate and DeMarco had already checked.

Missy sat on the edge of the bed like a woman waking up from a very bad dream, only to realize the dream was still taking place.

"You asked me earlier why he was in New York City," she said. "Jack worked as a senior accountant for a pretty big firm—Adler and Johnson. They've been working night and day on this big overhaul for a nuclear decommissioning company in South Carolina. On the really late nights, he's just been staying in the city."

"Were you expecting him back tonight or were you thinking he'd be staying in a hotel?" DeMarco asked.

"I talked to him at about seven this morning, before he left for his morning run. He said not only did he plan on being home today, but probably pretty early—maybe around four or so."

"I assume you started trying to call or text him at a certain point when you realized it was getting late?" Kate asked.

"Yeah, but not until seven or so. When those guys get deep into their jobs, time sort of goes out the window."

"Mrs. Tucker, the FBI was called in on your husband's murder because the situation reflects the details and circumstances of a case from eight years ago. The victim was another man who lived here in Ashton, also killed in New York," Kate explained. "There is no *hard* evidence to support it, but it's close enough to have alarmed the bureau. So it is very important that you try to think about any people that your husband might have made enemies with."

Kate could tell that Missy was once again fighting with tears. She gulped down the need to let out the grief, trying to get through it.

"I can't think of anyone. I'm not just saying it because I love the man, but he was extremely kind. Outside of a few little arguments at work, I don't think he ever had a heated argument his entire life."

"What about any close friends?" Kate asked. "Are there any friends, men in particular, that he hung around with who might have seen another side of him?"

"Well, he was a little silly with this group of friends out at the yacht club, but I don't think they'd describe him as anything negative."

"Do you have the names of some of these friends that we could talk to?" DeMarco asked.

"Yes. He had this core group…him and three other guys. They get together at the yacht club or hang out at the cigar bar and watch sports. Football, mostly."

"Do you happen to know if any of them have people they might consider enemies?" DeMarco asked. "Even jealous ex-wives or estranged family members?"

"I don't know. I don't know them that well and—"

The sound of uncontrollable sobbing from downstairs interrupted her. Missy looked in the direction of the bedroom door with a frown that made Kate's heart ache.

"That's Dylan, our middle child. He and his father were…"

She stopped here, her lip quivering as she tried to keep herself together.

"It's okay, Mrs. Tucker," DeMarco said. "Go to your kids. We've got enough to get started."

Missy got up quickly and sprinted for the door, already starting to cry. DeMarco followed behind her slowly, casting an angry look back at Kate. Kate stood in the bedroom a moment longer, getting a grip on her own emotions. No, this part of the job never got truly easier. And the fact that they had gotten very little information from the visit made it even worse.

She finally headed back out into the hallway, understanding why DeMarco was mad at her. Hell, she was a little angry with herself.

Kate walked back downstairs and head out the door. She saw that DeMarco was already getting into the car, wiping tears from her eyes. Kate closed the door softly behind her, the grief and weeping of the Tucker family pushing her along like an usher that led her deeper and deeper into a case that already seemed lost.

CHAPTER FOUR

By nine o'clock the following morning, news of Jack Tucker's murder had started making the rounds around Ashton. It was the main reason why it was so easy for Kate and DeMarco to get in touch with Jack's friends—the names and numbers of which Missy had given them last night. Not only had his friends already heard the news, they had started to come up with plans on how to help Missy and the kids as they dealt with their loss.

After a few quick phone calls, Kate and DeMarco had set up a meeting with three of Jack's friends at the yacht club. It was a Saturday, so the lot was already starting to fill up, even at nine in the morning. The club was located right along the Long Island Sound and had what Kate thought was probably the best view of the sound without all of the pretentious boat traffic getting in the way.

The club itself was a two-story building that looked nearly Colonial in style, with a modern twist, particularly to the exterior and landscaping. Kate was greeted by a man who was already standing at the doors. He was dressed in a simple button-down shirt and a pair of khakis—probably what passed for weekend casual for someone who belonged to a yacht club like this one.

"You Agent Wise?" the man asked.

"I am. And this is my partner, Agent DeMarco."

DeMarco only nodded, her anger and bitterness from the previous night still very much present. When they had parted ways at the hotel last night, DeMarco hadn't said so much as a single word. She *had* managed a simple "good morning" over their quick breakfast but that had been it so far.

"I'm James Cortez," the man said. "I spoke with you on the phone earlier this morning. The other guys are out on the veranda, ready and waiting with coffee."

He led them through the club, its high ceilings and warm environment utterly charming. Kate wondered how much it cost to be a member here for a year. Out of her price range for sure. When they stepped out onto the veranda that overlooked the Long Island Sound, she became certain of this. It was beautiful, looking directly out onto the water with the tall shapes and haze of the city on the other side.

There were two other men sitting at a small wooden table that held a large plate of pastries and bagels as well as a carafe of coffee. Both men looked up at the agents and got to their feet to greet them. One of the men looked rather young, certainly no older than thirty, while James Cortez and the other man were easily in their mid-forties.

"Duncan Ertz," the younger man said, extending his hand.

Kate and DeMarco both shook the men's hands as they went through a quick round of introductions. The older man was Paul Wickers, freshly retired from his job as a stockbroker and more than willing to talk about it, as it was the second thing that came out of his mouth.

Kate and DeMarco took a seat at the table. Kate took one of the empty coffee cups and filled it, doctoring it up with the sugar and cream that sat by the plate of breakfast pastries.

"It hurts to think about poor Missy and those kids this morning," Duncan said, biting into a Danish.

Kate recalled the trauma of last night and felt that she needed to check in on the poor woman. She looked across the table at DeMarco and wondered if she needed to check in on her, too. Removed from the situation, Kate was starting to understand that perhaps DeMarco had taken it so hard because of something in her past—something she had still not gotten over yet.

"Well," Kate said, "Missy specifically mentioned you gentlemen as those closest to Jack outside of his family. I was hoping to get some insights into the sort of man he was outside of his home and work."

"Well, that's the thing," James Cortez said. "From what I know, Jack was the same man no matter where he was. A straight shooter. A kind soul that always wanted to help others. If he had any flaws, I'd say it was that he was a little too involved with his work."

"He was always good for a joke," Duncan said. "They weren't funny most of the time, but he loved to tell them."

"That's for sure," Paul said.

"There were no secrets he told you guys about?" DeMarco asked. "Maybe an affair or even thoughts of an affair?"

"God no," Paul said. "Jack Tucker was insanely in love with his wife. I'd feel safe saying that man loved everything about his life. His wife, kids, work, friends…"

"That's why this makes no sense," James said. "I mean this in the most respectful way possible, but from an outsider's perspective, Jack was a pretty standard guy. Boring, almost."

"Any idea if he might have any connections to the victim of a murder that occurred eight years ago?" Kate asked. "A guy named Frank Nobilini who also lived in Ashton and was killed in New York."

"Frank Nobilini?" Duncan Ertz said, shaking his head.

"Yeah," James said. "Worked for that big-ass ad agency that does all the sneaker jobs. His wife was Jennifer…your wife probably knows her. Nice lady. Into community beautification projects and is very active with the PTA and things like that."

Ertz shrugged. Apparently, he was the newbie of the group and knew none of this.

"You think Jack's murder is linked to Nobilini's?" Paul asked.

"It's far too early to know that just yet," Kate said. "But given the nature of the murder, we have to look at it from that viewpoint."

"Do any of you happen to know the names of anyone Jack worked with?" DeMarco asked.

"There's only two people over him," Paul said. "One of them is a guy named Luca. He lives in Switzerland and comes over three or four times a year. The other is a local guy named Daiju Hiroto. I'm pretty sure he's the supervisor over the Adler and Johnson NYC offices."

"According to Jack," Duncan said, "Daiju is the kind of guy that practically lives at work."

"Was it common for Jack to have to work weekends?" Kate asked.

"Here and there," James said. "He'd done it a lot lately, actually. They're in the middle of some huge job to help bail out a nuclear decommissioning company. Last time I spoke with Jack, he said if they straightened it all out in time, there could be a *lot* of money involved in it."

"I'd bet good money you'll find almost the entire crew working today," Paul said. "They might be able to tell you some things we don't know about."

DeMarco slid one of her business cards over to James Cortez and then picked a cherry Danish from the plate in front of them. "Please give us a call if you think of anything else over the course of the next few days."

"And maybe keep the idea of the case from eight years ago to yourself," Kate said. "The last thing we need is for the people living in Ashton to get into a frenzy."

Paul nodded, sensing that she was speaking directly to him.

"Thanks, gentlemen," Kate said.

She took one more long sip of her coffee and left the men to their quiet breakfast. She glanced out at the sound where a sailboat was slowly coasting out into the water, as if tugging in the start of the weekend behind it.

"I'll get the address to Jack Tucker's office at Adler and Johnson," DeMarco said, pulling out her phone. And even in that, her tone was distant and cold.

She and I are going to have to hash this out before it gets out of hand, Kate thought. *Sure, she's a hard-ass but if I have to put her in her place, I won't hesitate to do so.*

***

The offices of Adler and Johnson were located in one of the more glamorous-looking high rises in Manhattan. It was located on the first and second floors of a building that also contained a law firm, a mobile applications developer, and a small literary agency. As it turned out, Paul Wickers had been correct; most of the team Jack Tucker had worked with was in the office. The workspace smelled of strong coffee and though there was a great deal of busyness among the eight people working, there was a somber mood as well.

Daiju Hiroto met with them right away, escorting them into his large office. He looked like a man torn—perhaps between his need to get this massive project finished on time and the humane reaction to the death of a co-worker and friend.

"I learned the news this morning," Hiroto said from behind his large desk. "I had been at work since six this morning and one of our workers—Katie Mayer—came in with the news. There were fifteen of us here at the time and I gave them all the option of taking the weekend off. Six people thought it best to leave to pay their respects."

"If you did not have this team to oversee, would you have done the same?" Kate asked.

"No. It is a selfish answer, but this job has to be done. We have two weeks to finish everything and we are a bit behind. And more than fifty people's jobs are at risk if we don't pull it off."

"Of your team, who do you think would have known Jack the best?" Kate asked.

"Probably me. Jack and I worked very closely together on several large jobs over the last ten years or so. We've traveled all over the world together and pulled late nights and meetings that the rest of the team didn't even know about."

"But you said someone else knew about his death first?" DeMarco asked.

"Yes, Katie. She lives in Ashton and is fairly good friends with Jack's wife."

Kate wanted to say something about how it seemed a little offensive that Hiroto was not calling it a day so that he, as well as the others who had dutifully stayed behind, could grieve. But she knew the demons that sometimes drove men who were possessed by their work and knew that it was not her place to make such a judgment.

"In all of your time with Jack, did you ever know him to keep secrets?" DeMarco asked.

"Not that I can think of. And if he did, I apparently wasn't someone he wished to divulge them to. But between the three of us, I find it very hard to believe that Jack had a secret life. He was on the straight and narrow, you know? A good guy. Polished around the edges."

"So you can't think of any reason someone might have wanted to kill him?" Kate asked.

"No. The idea is insane." He paused here and looked out through the glass walls of his office and to the rest of his team. "And it was here in the city?" he asked.

"It was. Did you not call him when you realized he had not come in?"

"Oh, I did. Several times. When he didn't answer by noon or so, I let it go. Jack was always very sharp, very smart. If he needed a few hours just to get away—which he did from time to time—I let him have it."

"Mr. Hiroto, would you mind if we spoke to some of the others out there?" Kate asked, nodding toward the other side of the glass walls.

"By all means. Help yourself."

"And could you get the contact information of those that decided to leave?" DeMarco asked.

"Certainly."

Kate and DeMarco ventured out into the workspace of cubicles, large desks, and rich coffee. But even before they had spoken to a single person, Kate got a pretty good feeling that they were going to get more of the same. Usually, when more than one person described someone else as being very plain and uneventful, it usually turned out to be true.

Within fifteen minutes, they had spoken with the eight other workers currently in the office. Kate had been right; everyone described Jack and sweet, kind, not one to rock the boat. And for the second time that morning, someone referred to Jack Tucker as boring—but in a good, non-offensive way.

In the back of her head, Kate felt something stir, some memory or saying that she had heard somewhere along the roads of her life. Something about watching out for a bored wife or spouse—how the boredom might make them snap. But it wouldn't come to her.

After stopping by Hiroto's office one last time to get a list of the people who had elected to leave work, Kate and DeMarco headed back out into the gorgeous New York City Saturday morning. She thought of poor Missy Tucker, sitting under the weight of this beautiful day, trying to adapt to a life that, for a while anyway, might not seem so beautiful at all.

***

They spent the rest of their morning visiting with the ones who had decided to leave work. They encountered many tears and even a few who were enraged that a man as innocent and as kind as Jack Tucker would have been murdered. It was exactly the same as speaking to the others in the office, only not as stifling.

They spoke with the last person—a man named Jerry Craft—shortly after lunchtime. They arrived at his home just as Jerry was getting into his car. Kate parked behind him in his driveway, catching an irritated look. She stepped out of the car as Jerry Craft approached them. His eyes were red and he looked quite melancholy.

"Sorry to bother you," Kate said, showing her ID. DeMarco stepped up beside her and did the same. "We're agents Wise and DeMarco, FBI. We were hoping you might have some time to speak with us about Jack Tucker."

The irritation quickly left Jerry's face and he nodded and propped himself up against the back of his car.

"I don't know what I could offer than what I'm sure you've already heard from everyone else. I assume you spoke with Mr. Hiroto and everyone else at the office?"

"We have," Kate said. "We're now speaking with those that left today—as it would seem they had a closer connection with Jack."

"I don't know if that's necessarily true," Jerry said. "There were only a few of us that ever really hung out outside of work. And Jack usually wasn't among them. A few of them probably took Hiroto up on his offer just to get a day off."

"Any idea why Jack wasn't one to hang out after work hours?" DeMarco asked.

"No reason, I don't think. Jack was something of a home body, you know? He'd rather be at home with his wife and kids in his free time. The job had him working crazy hours as it was—no sense in hanging at a bar with those same people you just left work with. He loved his family, you know? Always doing extravagant things for birthdays and anniversaries. Always talking up his kids at work."

"So you also think he had the perfect life?" Kate asked.

"Seemed that way. Although, really, can any of us have a *perfect* life? I mean, even Jack had some strain with his mother from what I know. But don't we all?"

"How's that?"

"Nothing big. There was this one day at work where I heard him talking to his wife on the phone. He was out in the stairwell for privacy, but I was using one of the older workstations right by the stairwell door. It stands out because it was the only time I heard him speaking to or about his wife with anything but happiness in his voice."

"And it was a conversation about his mother?" Kate asked.

"Pretty sure. I sort of teased him about it when he came back in but he wasn't in a joking mood."

"Do you know anything about his parents?" Kate asked.

"No. Like I said, Jack was a great guy, but I wouldn't really call him a *friend*."

"Where are you headed right now?" DeMarco asked.

"I was going to go grab some flowers for his family and drop them by their house. I met his wife and kids a few times at Christmas parties and company barbecues, things like that. A great little family. It's a damned shame what happened. Makes me a little sick, you know?"

"Well, we won't keep you any longer," Kate said. "Thank you, Mr. Craft."

Back in the car, Kate backed out of Jerry's driveway and said: "You want to grab Jack's mother's information?"

"On it," DeMarco said a little coldly.

Kate again found herself fighting to stay quiet. If DeMarco was going to draw out her little irritation about last night's events, that was her choice. Kate sure as hell wasn't going to let it affect her progress on this case.

At the same time, she also found herself having to bite back an ironic smile. She had spent so much time wrestling with whether or not her new position was keeping her away from her family yet here she was, working with a woman who reminded her so much of Melissa at times that it was scary. She thought of Melissa and Michelle as DeMarco was bounced back and forth along the departments within the bureau, searching for information on Jack Tucker's mother. She thought of how Melissa had behaved and acted the first time she, Kate, had been so enthralled in the Nobilini case. That had been eight years ago; Melissa had been twenty-one, still slightly rebellious and pretty much against anything her mother wished of her. There had been one stretch of time where Melissa had tried out coloring her hair purple. It had actually looked quite good but Kate had never been able to bring herself to say it out loud. It had been a trying time in their lives, even when Michael, her husband, had still been alive and there to help her do the parenting as Melissa had gotten older.

"That's interesting," DeMarco said, pulling Kate out of her trip down memory lane. She was setting her phone down and looking ahead with an excited little sparkle in her eyes.

"What's interesting?" Kate asked.

"Jack's mother is one Olivia Tucker. Sixty-six years old, lives in Queens. A squeaky clean criminal record, but with one minor ding."

"What's the ding?"

"She had the cops called on her two years ago. The call was placed by Missy Tucker, on the same night Olivia Tucker was trying to force her way into their house."

They shared a look and in it, Kate could feel some of that tension between them start to melt away. Good leads, after all, had a tendency to bring even the most estranged partners together.

Feeling as if she was finally getting somewhere, Kate turned the car around and headed toward Queens.

CHAPTER FIVE

Olivia Tucker lived in a basic run-of-the-mill apartment in Jackson Heights. When Kate and DeMarco arrived, she was being visited by a local preacher. It was the preacher who answered the door, a tall black man who looked very somber and sad. He regarded the agents skeptically and sighed softly.

"Can I help you ladies?"

"We need to speak with Mrs. Tucker," DeMarco said. "Who might you be?"

"I'm Leland Toombs, the pastor of her church. And who might you be?"

They went through the usual routine of showing their IDs and introducing themselves. Toombs took a tentative step back and gave them a disapproving look.

"You understand she is in a very distressed state, right?"

"Of course," Kate said. "We're trying to find her son's killer and we are hoping she might be able to shed some light to help."

"Who is that?" a shaky voice called from elsewhere in the apartment. A woman stepped into view from another room and started for the door.

"It's the FBI," Leland told her. "But Olivia, I'd suggest you take a moment to think about if you are ready to speak with them."

Olivia Tucker came to the door looking an absolute mess. Her eyes were bloodshot and it looked like she was even having trouble walking. She looked at Kate and DeMarco and then placed a reassuring hand on Toombs's shoulder.

"Yes, I think I need to," she said. "Pastor Toombs, would you give me a moment?"

"I think maybe I should be here when they speak with you."

She shook her head. "No. I appreciate it, but I need to do this part on my own."

Toombs frowned and then looked at Kate and DeMarco. "Please be kind. She is not taking this well." He then gave Olivia one final look and stepped out of the door while calling over his shoulder, "Please call me if you need anything, Olivia."

Olivia watched him go and then slowly closed the door behind her. "Please, come on into the living room."

25

Her voice was soft and ragged and she still walked as if her legs weren't quite sure what they were doing.

"Did you know," she said as they entered the living room, "that the cops called me and told me what had happened a full six hours after his body was found?"

"Why so long?" Kate asked.

"I suppose they assumed Missy would call and tell me. They told her first, of course. But it was later, after Missy had refused, that the police finally called."

"Are you sure she *refused*?" DeMarco asked. "Given the nature of what happened, do you think she simply forgot?"

Olivia shrugged, but not as an *I don't know* gesture. It was more of an *I don't care.*

"Do you mean to tell me that you think Missy would have done something like that on purpose?" Kate asked.

"Honestly, I just don't know. The woman is vindictive as hell. I wouldn't put much of anything beyond her. She probably *forgot* so she wouldn't have to speak to me or, God forbid, *see* me."

"Want to tell us why you seem to dislike her so much?" DeMarco asked.

"Oh, I never liked her, not really. She was quite charming at first, when she was trying to earn my good graces. But the moment Jack put that engagement ring on her finger, she became some other person. Controlling. Manipulative. She has never appreciated the plush little life she has. She may have loved Jack deep down in some sick, twisted way—I don't doubt that. But she never appreciated him."

"Can you explain that a bit more?" Kate asked.

"She was always wanting something else—wanting more. And she made no secret of it. Everything she had, no matter what it was—kids, wealthy husband, beautiful house, you name it—it was never enough. Nothing Jack ever did was good enough for her."

Kate noticed the look of absolute venom in Olivia's face as she spoke. She believed every single word she was saying. But from the little bit of time Kate had spent with Missy Tucker, she found it all very hard to believe.

"Do you know if Jack felt this way about her?"

"God, no. He was so blinded by it all. By her and her little act."

"So you'd comfortably rule out the idea of him being involved in an affair?"

Her look of shock was all the answer Kate needed. But Olivia had some choice words, too. "Given what I've been through the last few hours, how dare you ask such a stupid question? Are you *trying* to be insensitive and rude?"

"I ask only because that would at least give us somewhere to start looking. If he was involved in something like that, it would give us a series of leads to pursue. Because quite frankly, as of now, we have no witnesses and no suspects."

"Suspects? Honey, I've already told you who did it. It was his hateful wife."

Kate and DeMarco shared an uneasy glance. Whether Oliva Tucker's statement was true or not, this case was going to get quite awkward before it was brought to a close.

Kate let the comment hang in the air for a moment before going on. When she did, she was sure to use her words carefully, choosing each one with great purpose.

"Are you sure you want to make such a bold statement?" Kate asked. "If you're serious about that, I have to consider it a lead and start pursuing Missy Tucker as a potential suspect."

"You do your job the way you want," Olivia said. "But I know that woman. She wanted something different. She wanted out, but without the risk of losing everything in the process. Now you tell me some easier way to go about doing that than killing your husband."

Throughout all of her career, Kate didn't think she'd ever met anyone who was so blinded with hatred for someone else—in-laws, estranged siblings, and so on, she'd seen it all. But Olivia Tucker took things to a whole different level.

"I have to point out," DeMarco said, "that a great deal of time on our trip out here was spent going over everything there was to know about both Jack *and* Missy. While we don't have full reports by any means, there was more than enough to see that there was no marital discord strong enough to ping any legal issues."

"That's right," Kate said. "Additionally, there were no financial troubles, no marks on her criminal record, nothing like that. You, on the other hand, do have a slight mark on your record. Do you want to tell me about the night Missy had to call the cops because you were trying to get into their home?"

"Jack was having a hard time at work. He'd had a panic attack. I called to check on him and to talk to my grandkids, but Missy wasn't allowing it. She told me that Jack was too nice to say anything, but that *I* was part of the reason for his panic attack. She hung up on me when I called so I decided to go to their house. We had it out and she shoved me out the door, refusing to let me into the house. After that…well, I let my temper get the best of me and she called the police."

"If we need to, we'll look into that," Kate said "But honestly, there is nothing we have seen and nothing in the records to indicate that Missy would have had any reason at all to kill her husband. There's no motive that we can see."

"Well, if you're that convinced, why the hell are you even here to speak with me?"

"Honestly?" DeMarco said. "It's because your name came up. One of Jack's co-workers overheard him having a heated conversation with his wife about you. We checked your records just to cover our bases and found out about the police call."

Olivia smiled the sort of smile often seen on tired villains in movies. "Well then, it seems you already have your mind made up about me."

"That's not the case at all. We just—"

"If you ladies don't mind, I'm going to politely ask you to leave. I'd like to properly grieve my son."

Kate knew that their time with Olivia Tucker was over; if she kept pressing, the woman would only shut down. Besides that, she had been useless for information—unless the vile feelings she had toward her daughter-in-law could be seen as truth. And Kate doubted there was anything to it.

"Thank you," Kate said. "And we are truly sorry for your loss."

Olivia nodded, got up, and walked out of the room. "I'm sure you remember where the door is," she said, before disappearing elsewhere into the house.

Kate and DeMarco took their leave, no closer to a solid lead but having been thoroughly rattled by Olivia Tucker's views on Missy.

"You think there's a shred of truth to any of it?" DeMarco asked. She seemed to be coming out of her funk, apparently motivated by the case.

"I think in this moment, while she's searching for answers to what happened, she thinks some of it is true. I think she's taking little nuggets of fears she's had over the years and amplifying them just to have some object to place her blame and rage on."

DeMarco nodded as they got into the car. "Whatever it was, it was ugly."

"And I think it rules her out of any foul play. We may want to keep an eye on Missy, though, just to keep her safe. Maybe even let local PD know how unhinged Olivia seems to be."

"And then what?"

"And then we regroup. Possibly over a glass or two of wine back at the hotel."

It sounded like a good idea but Kate continued to think of Missy Tucker and how her world was now very much an empty shell of what it had once been. Kate remembered all too well what it felt like to lose the man you loved, the man who knew you like a book he'd read millions of times. It was heartbreaking beyond words and drained the life out of you.

Revisiting that feeling in that moment, as she headed toward the hotel, made her more motivated that ever. It made her reach back into her memories to where details of the first case rested, back where the Nobilini case had started.

Her mind tried to latch onto a name—a name she knew well but that had faded into the deeper regions of her memory. It was a name she was reminded of earlier in the day, when they had met with Jack Tucker's friends at the yacht club.

Cass Nobilini.

You know there are answers there, Kate thought.

There might be. And she'd go looking for them if it came to that.

But she really hoped it wouldn't. She hoped she could make it the rest of her life never seeing Cass Nobilini again. But she also knew the chances of that were very slim—that she may, in fact, be seeing her sooner rather than later.

CHAPTER SIX

They settled in at the hotel's bar just as the dinner rush started to pack the place out. While the prospect of a glass of wine was indeed promising, Kate found that she was a bit more excited about the burger she ordered. Usually when on a case, she'd somehow forget to eat lunch, leaving her ravenous at the end of the day. As she sank her mouth into the burger for the first bite, she saw DeMarco giving her a small smile. It was her first authentic smile of the day.

"What?" Kate asked through a mouthful of burger.

"Nothing," DeMarco said, picking at her grilled chicken salad. "It's reassuring to see a woman of your size and age eat like that."

Swallowing down the bite, Kate nodded and said, "I was gifted with an amazing metabolism."

"Oh, what a bitch."

"It's worth it to be able to eat like this."

A brief silence passed between them, which was shattered by both of them laughing together at the exchange. It felt good to be able to lower her guard around DeMarco after the tense day they'd shared. DeMarco seemed to feel the same way, based on what she said after sipping from her glass of wine.

"Sorry I was so bitter all day. The whole thing of breaking news like that to a family…it's hard. I mean, I know it's hard, but it's especially hard on me. I had this thing happen in my past that jarred me. I thought I was over it, but apparently, I'm not."

"What happened?"

DeMarco took a moment, perhaps considering whether or not she wanted to delve into the story. With another large sip of wine, she decided to go ahead with it. She let out a sigh and began.

"I knew I was gay when I was fourteen. I had my first girlfriend when I was sixteen. When I was seventeen, my girlfriend Rose and I—she was nineteen—decided that we were going to go ahead and come out. We both had kept it a secret, particularly from our parents. So there we were—about to break the news. I was supposed to meet her at her house and we were going to tell her parents, who, I might add, assumed that Rose and I were just really good friends. I was always at her house and vice versa, you know? So I'm sitting there on her parents' couch when I get a phone call.

It's from the police, telling me that Rose was in a car accident and that she had died right away, upon impact. I was called rather than her parents because they found her cell phone and saw that I took up about ninety percent of her call history.

"So I break down right away and her parents are sitting there, wondering what the hell happened—why I'm suddenly in tears, on my knees in the floor. And I had to tell them. I had to tell them what the policeman had just told me." She paused here, poked at her salad a bit, and then added, "It was the absolute worst moment of my life."

Kate found it hard to look at DeMarco; she was delivering the story not as an emotional part of it, but as if she were a robot, reciting back a series of events. Still, the tale was more than enough to explain DeMarco's attitude the previous night when she, Kate, had volunteered them to break the bad news to Missy Tucker.

"If I'd known any of that, you know I wouldn't have volunteered us," Kate said.

"I know. And I knew it then. But my emotions strangled any reason or logic. Quite honestly, I just needed to sit and stew in it for a while. Sorry you caught the brunt of it."

"Water under the bridge," Kate said.

"Have you done that a lot in your career? Breaking news like that?"

"Oh yes. And it never gets easy. It becomes easier to detach yourself from it, but the act itself is never easy."

The table fell into silence again. The waiter came by and refilled their wine as Kate continued to work on her burger.

"So how's your man?" DeMarco asked. "Allen, right?"

"He's doing good. He's just about to the point in the relationship where he worries about me still being involved in the FBI. He'd prefer that I take a desk job. Or stay retired."

"So it's getting serious, huh?"

"It feels that way. And part of me is excited for it. But there's a small part of me that feels like it would be a waste of time. He and I are both quickly approaching sixty. Starting a new relationship at that age feels...odd, I guess." Sensing that DeMarco would latch onto the topic if she was allowed to do so, Kate quickly redirected the conversation.

"How about you? Has the love life picked up at all since the last time we had this awkward conversation?"

DeMarco shook her head and smiled. "No, but that's by choice. I'm still enjoying the Land of One-Night Stands while I still can."

"Does that make you happy?"

DeMarco seemed genuinely shocked by the question. "It sort of does. I don't need the responsibilities and requirements that come with a relationship right now."

Kate chuckled. She had never been in the Land of One-Night Stands. She'd met Michael while in college and married him a year and a half later. It had been the kind of relationship where she had started to understand that they would spend their lives together as soon as their first kiss.

"So where's the next step in this case?" DeMarco asked.

"I'm thinking about revisiting the initial case rather than just using it as a reference. I'm wondering if there's new information that might have come up within the Nobilini family. But...well, like your story about your girlfriend being killed while you sat on her parents' sofa, it's not territory that is easily ventured back into."

"So more awkward visits and conversations tomorrow?"

"Maybe. I'm not sure yet."

"Is there anything worth filling me in on before I step blindly into it?"

"Probably. But trust me...it would be better saved for the morning. Going into it right now is only going to keep us up late and screw with my sleep."

"Oh. *Those* kinds of stories."

"Exactly."

They finished their current glasses of wine and paid their checks. On the way up to their rooms, Kate thought about the story DeMarco had just told—of that sad glimpse into her past. It made her very aware that she knew very little about her partner. If they were working in a normal relationship, seeing one another nearly every day rather than once or twice every few months, that would certainly be different. It made her wonder if she was doing her part to truly get to know DeMarco.

They parted ways at their rooms—Demarco's directly across the hall from Kate's—and Kate felt the need to say something. Anything, really, to let her know that she appreciated DeMarco's willingness to open up.

"Again, I apologize about last night. It's dawning on me that I don't know you well enough to be making decisions like that for both of us."

"It's fine, really," DeMarco said. "I should have told you about it last night."

"We need to be intentional about getting to know one another. If we're trusting each other with our lives, it's kind of necessary. Maybe outside of work sometime."

"Yeah, that would be nice." DeMarco paused here as she opened her door. "You said you had some thinking to do…about the old case. The Nobilini case. Let me know if you need someone to ping ideas off of."

"I'll do that," Kate said.

With that, they entered the rooms, ending the day between them. Kate kicked off her shoes and went directly to her laptop. As she booted it up, she called Director Duran. As she'd expected, he did not answer his phone but the line was then redirected to his assistant director, a woman named Nancy Saunders. Kate put in a request to have digital copies of the Nobilini files sent to her email as soon as possible. She knew that DeMarco had brought a few, but it was just the overview of the case. Kate felt the need to get back into the grittiness of the case, right down to the finer details. Saunders committed to getting it done, letting her know she'd have them by nine o'clock the following morning.

Cass Nobilini, Kate thought.

She'd thought of the woman almost right away, after Duran had told her about the possible connection. She'd thought of her again when she'd heard the wails and screeches of Missy Tucker as she grieved her murdered husband, and then again while talking to Jack Tucker's friends.

Cass Nobilini, the mother of Frank Nobilini. The woman who had found it insulting and darkly improper for the media to latch onto the event of her son's murder just because he had once worked closely with a few popular men in Congress as a financial advisor. Kate felt that she had been a fool to even pretend that this case was not going to lead her back to Cass Nobilini in some way.

It was that thought that remained with her for the remainder of the night, clinging to the forefront of her mind as she eventually lay down in bed and drifted off to sleep.

***

She could still see the crime scene in her head. The wear and tear of memory made it a little faded and rusty, but the haziness was stripped away whenever she dreamed about it. In her dreams, it was as clear as if she were watching television.

And she saw it that night, managing to fall asleep shortly after nine yet twitching and moaning slightly in her sleep as the midnight hour approached.

The scene: Frank Nobilini, killed in the alley and still holding his BMW keys. The case had eventually led her back to his home, a four-bedroom house in Ashton. She'd started in the garage, which had smelled faintly of lawn trimmings from a recent grass-cutting. She'd felt like she was in some haunted place, like Frank Nobilini's spirit was there somewhere, waiting for her. Maybe in the empty space where his BMW was supposed to be but, at that time, had sat in a parking lot several blocks away from where his body had been found. The garage had been cold and like some weird tomb. It was one of the handful of scenes from her past that always came back vividly for reasons she had never understood.

There had been no clues of any kind at the house, no signs of why someone might want to kill him. One would think that maybe it was for his very nice car, but the keys had been in his hand. The house had been clean. Almost eerily so. No paperwork trails, nothing of note in the address books or the mail. Nothing.

In her dream, Kate was standing there, in the alley. She was touching the still-sticky smear of gore on side of the wall in the same experimental way a child might touch a stray drop of syrup on the kitchen table. She turned and looked behind her, wanting to look down the alleyway, but saw the interior of the Nobilinis' garage instead. As if she had been invited inside, she walked to the wooden stairs that led to the door that would take her into the kitchen. She then moved in the way that only dreams allow, fluidly, almost being projected rather than moved by her legs. She somehow ended up in the bathroom, looking to the large tub/shower combo installed in the wall. It was filled with blood. Something was moving beneath the surface, causing little bubbles to rise to the top of the blood. When one would pop, it would send tiny droplets against the porcelain side of the wall.

She backed away, stepping through the bathroom doorway and into the hall. There, Frank Nobilini was walking toward her. Behind him, his wife, Jennifer, simply watched. She even gave Kate a harmless little wave as her dead husband lurched down the hallway. Frank walked very zombie-like, slowly and with an exaggerated gait.

"It's okay," someone said from behind her.

She turned and saw Cass Nobilini, Frank's mother, sitting on the floor. She looked tired, defeated...as if she were waiting for an executioner's blade.

"Cass...?"

"You were never going to solve it. It was over your head. But time...it has a way of changing things, doesn't it?"

Kate turned back to Frank, still advancing. As he came by the bathroom door, Kate saw that some of the blood had come out of the tub and into the floor, seeping out into the hallway. When Frank stepped in it, it made a wet sucking sound.

Frank Nobilini smiled at her and raised his hand to her—slightly decayed and mottled. Kate slowly backed away, raising her own hands to her face, and let out a scream.

She woke up, feeling the scream lodged in her throat.

That damned house. She had never understood why it had rattled her in such a way. Maye because of Jennifer Nobilini's screams and wails, laced with the picture-perfect house…it had all seemed surreal. Like something out of an artsy horror movie.

Kate sat up and slowly inched her way to the edge of the bed. She collected a few deep breaths and looked at the clock: 1:22. The only light in the room came from the numbers on the alarm clock and the faint glow of the security lights outside, barely shining in through the closed blinds.

She'd had dreams concerning Cass Nobilini and that first case before, but this one had been a doozy. Her heart was still hammering in her chest as she got out of bed and walked to the mini-fridge for a bottle of water. She sipped some down as she walked over to the bedside table where she had set her laptop up.

She flicked on the bedside lamp and logged into her email. She had only one new one, and that had come from Assistant Director Saunders. She'd tasked an agent with digging up the Nobilini files and they had been delivered to her shortly before midnight.

She knew that there was no way she'd return to a deep sleep, so she opened them up one by one, a bit uncomfortable by how natural it seemed and how familiar those old files felt. She looked through them briefly at first, in the same way someone visiting a somewhat familiar location might give the area a once-over before truly starting to study the place. When she came to the last of the twenty-six pages, she went back to the beginning. But before getting deep into it, she went to the little complimentary coffee maker and set a pot to brew. As it started to percolate, she made the bed, relocated the laptop to the small table against the far wall, and made herself a little workstation.

Within five minutes, she was reading each of the files line by line and sipping on a cup of very dark, very cheap coffee. The account of Frank Nobilini felt like an old friend, the sort of friend that only called with bad news. The case detailed every conversation she'd had with neighbors and friends in Ashton. As she read over them all, she was unsettled with how similar they all were to the conversations she'd recently had concerning Jack Tucker.

The only thing that had even remotely resembled anything of merit had come from twenty-two-year-old Alice Delgado, a nanny for a family in Ashton who had cared for two kids, ages eight and eleven. Alice had admitted to making sexual advances toward Frank Nobilini when they had crossed paths at a local park. Frank had responded with flattery and polite rejection. While that had been the extent of it, the news of Frank's death had made Alice feel incredibly guilty—so guilty that she had contacted Jennifer Nobilini to confess. Jennifer, the caring and apparently flawless woman she was, had forgiven her almost right away.

Aside from that one detail, there had been nothing. Not in conversations, not at the crime scene, not in the Nobilinis' home. And nothing in the criminal records for Frank or Jennifer—no history of criminal activities, no enemies to speak of…nothing.

Kate had remained on the case for six months, then took a step back, working on it only as a background project for another eight months before the case was totally given up on. It had not been the only unsolved case in her career, but it *had* been the only unclosed case with such a degree of strangeness to it.

As she read through, she did her best to apply Jack Tucker's death to it. And the more she read and reacquainted herself with the case, the more certain she became that Jack's murder was linked. It was either done by the exact same killer or a copycat.

It was 4:10 before she felt she had given the notes and files their proper attention. She stared at her second cup of coffee for a moment and then slowly picked up her cell phone. She placed a call to the twenty-four/seven resource line at the bureau. It was a bit slower than a direct call to Saunders or Duran during the day but it was better than nothing.

After giving her name and badge number, she was greeted by a voice that was far too warm and pleasant for a quarter after four in the morning.

"Agent Wise, how can we help you?"

"I need the current address and phone number for a woman that probably lives somewhere in New York. Cass Nobilini."

"Okay, and is this going to be the best number to send that information to?"

"It is. Thanks."

But even before she ended the call, Kate felt guilty as hell. There was a very large part of her that hoped Cass Nobilini had decided to move. If Kate could make it through this case without having to cross paths with Cass, she'd consider herself fortunate.

You know that won't happen, Kate thought. *You're just not that lucky.*

She got her answer twenty minutes later when she got a return call from the bureau. After giving the phone number for one Cass Nobilini, the address confirmed it.

"127 Harper Street. Ashton, New York."

CHAPTER SEVEN

Kate was wired on nerves and late-night coffee as she and DeMarco loaded up into the car the following morning. They'd had a quick complimentary breakfast within the hotel before leaving, but Kate had not been able to eat much. Her stomach felt even more unstable as she pulled the car out into Sunday morning traffic, realizing that she was going to have to try to explain her history with Cass Nobilini to DeMarco.

"Here's the thing," Kate said. "I don't want you feeling like I'm keeping things from you and I certainly don't want you to feel like I'm expecting you to go into this blindly. So I need to tell you about Cass Nobilini. I need to tell you how, even above the unsolved murder of her son, dealing with her was the hardest part of this case."

"Was she confrontational?" DeMarco asked.

"No. Not quite. But...well, it's hard to explain."

"We've got a twenty-minute drive out to Ashton. Try."

Kate knew she had to get it out—if not to inform DeMarco, then to simply expel it from her mind so it would quit nagging at her. She was pleased to find that once she got started, it really wasn't that difficult at all.

"Eight years ago, when Frank Nobilini was killed, I met Cass Nobilini—Frank's mother. She had been told the news about a day or so before the FBI arrived. She was grieving, sure, but she was also...*determined*. That's the best word I can think to use. She was determined to figure out who had killed her son. She was extremely helpful when we spoke with her but as far as she was concerned, everyone was a suspect. Everyone from the guy that got his order wrong at the deli to the mailman. I wish I was exaggerating here, DeMarco, but I'm not. She would call at least four or five times a day to ask me if I had considered someone in particular. And the longer we went without finding a killer, the more persistent she became. The more time that went by without us coming up with a suspect, the more insistent she became that she could figure it out herself...that we were very bad at our jobs. And because I was the lead on it, I got the brunt of it all."

"Was it like a coping mechanism?" DeMarco.

38

"That's what the bureau psychiatrist said. And honestly, it's not that uncommon in cases where the death is sudden and the killer is never found. But Cass went above and beyond. There was one day where I had to sit down with her and get a little mean; I had to tell her to back off and let the bureau do their job. She responded in an honest way, telling us that if we were doing our jobs the right way, we'd have her son's killer in custody.

"She obeyed for the most part, though. At first. When we were quietly taken off of the case and just sort of had it running the background, I got a call one night. A call from Cass Nobilini. This was about five months after we'd stopped running hard after the case. She called me and told me that she knew who had killed her son. She said the FBI needed to come back to Ashton. And I had to tell her the truth—that unless she had hard evidence to support her claims, the bureau couldn't become active on it again. Of course, she never had that evidence. So she called me one more time a few weeks later to let me know that she would forever blame the FBI—me, in particular, as the lead agent on the case—for not bringing her son's killer to justice."

"That's a little unfair," DeMarco said.

"It is. And unrealistic, too. But for some reason, that always stuck with me. At the risk of sounding like a diva, I always took failure very hard. The fact that I could never find such a blatant killer *and* was being blamed by a mother of the victim for never finding the killer...well, that's haunted me for years."

"And we're about to pay her a visit," DeMarco said. She rubbed at her head and gave a lopsided grin. "Now I feel *really* bad for giving you such a hard time about Missy Tucker. Did you call ahead?"

"No. I probably should have. But I didn't want to give her any warning. I have no clue how she'll respond to seeing me."

"Since she lives in Ashton, I'd assume she's already heard about the murder. Any chance you think she might be *expecting* you to show up?"

To that, Kate had no answer. What she didn't dare say, though, was that she was actually hoping Cass Nobilini would not be home.

***

It was the same house Kate had been inside eight years ago. She was pretty sure the porch had been repainted and that most of the landscaping was new, but it was eerily familiar otherwise. As she and DeMarco stepped up onto the porch steps, Kate felt a little

39

foolish at the fact that her heart seemed to be trying to beat right out of her chest.

"You good?" DeMarco asked.

Before she could even think about the answer, Kate knocked on the door with a hard, rapid motion.

Almost right away, there was a response from inside, a sing-song *"Coming! One second!"*

The past came roaring back to Kate. Being blamed for not finding the killer, having to tell Cass to calm the hell down and stay out of the way of the FBI. It all hit her as she heard the footfalls approaching and for a moment, she nearly wanted to make a run for it. But then the door was opening in front of them and a woman straight out of Kate's past looked out at them. Most of her hair was now gray and there was an abundance of wrinkles on her seventy-year-old face, but she looked remarkably upbeat, all things considered.

It was clear that Cass recognized her right away. She looked from Kate to DeMarco and then back to Kate. The slow smile that crept onto her face seemed genuine enough.

"Agent Wise," Cass said. "It's...well, I guess it's nice to see you."

"You, too."

"I thought you'd show up sooner or later. You're here in town about Jack Tucker, I take it?"

"Yes."

Cass nodded and let out a sigh. She stared at Kate for a moment, just long enough for a thick tension to worm its way back into Kate's heart.

"Well, come on in," she said. "I've got some cinnamon rolls that just came out of the oven. And coffee ready to go."

Cass led them into the house, walking casually ahead of them. The smell of freshly baked cinnamon rolls beckoned like a ghostly finger, pulling them forward.

"Looks like you were right," Kate whispered softly to DeMarco as they walked down the hallway. "It *is* almost as if she was expecting me. I'm a sucker for a good cinnamon roll."

Cass led them into her kitchen. Kate thought it, like some of the exterior of the house, had seen some TLC since the last time she visited. As she perched herself on a barstool along the kitchen counter, the entire scene from eight years ago flashed in her head.

I was standing, leaning against the counter by the stove, when Cass nearly fainted from the grief of losing her son. Her husband

40

had died two years earlier. Prostate cancer. She cried out to him in her anguish and pleaded with me to explain it all to her.

Kate shook the thought away, not allowing herself to go back there. Besides, Cass looked well. Perhaps whatever skewed motivations had pushed her all those years ago had died. Maybe she was now a perfectly healthy and rational woman. Time healed all wounds, right?

"Mrs. Nobilini, this is—" Kate started.

"Oh, I think you and I have been through enough where you can call me Cass."

With a smile, Kate tried again. "Cass, this is my partner, Agent DeMarco. I've informed her of our history."

"All of it?" Cass asked as she took cinnamon rolls out of a still-steaming pan and placed them on plates she took from the cupboard.

"Yes. Even the things you probably wouldn't want a stranger to know."

Cass nodded as she brought the agents each a cinnamon roll. "I'm not particularly proud of that time of my life. I dealt with my pain in sorrow in some very questionable ways. I always meant to call you...to apologize..."

"It's okay," Kate said. "How are you?"

"I'm okay now. But that period went on for years. I...well, I nearly broke the law a few times if I'm being honest. Surveilling people, coming close to breaking and entering a few times." She sat down on the other side of the bar on her own stool and joined them with her own roll. "I devoted my life to it for several months. The final straw was when close friends of mine called the police on me. Not for breaking any laws, but because they feared I was a danger to myself. I went to therapy and worked it all out."

Kate wasn't sure what to say. She couldn't imagine going through that sort of pain, even after losing her own husband several years ago to dubious circumstances.

"Well, as you said at the door," DeMarco said, apparently sensing Kate's hesitation, "we're in the area to try to solve another murder. Jack Tucker. A murder that seems to be eerily similar to your son's."

"Can I ask how similar?" Cass asked. But her tone indicated she might not be prepared to hear it.

"Same type of gun. Same execution style. Another resident of Ashton who appears to have been a very happily married man with a perfect life, found in an alleyway in New York City."

"My God," Cass said.

41

"I wonder, though," Kate said. "In all of that time you spent working towards trying to find answers, did you come across *anything* that, even now, felt like it might lead somewhere?"

"No. Nothing." Cass looked away, poking at her cinnamon roll in embarrassment. "And after a while, it occurred to me that anyone that was able to kill Frank in such a blatant and egregious way…well, they're probably long gone by now."

"It would be a reasonable thing to assume," Kate said. "In terms of Jack Tucker, did you know him or his family by any chance?"

"I didn't personally," she said. "But something occurred to me yesterday that seems odd. It might be nothing, but…it doesn't feel like it."

"What's that?" Kate asked.

"Do you remember Alice Delgado?"

The name popped up in her head as if it had been waiting all along. The fact that she had revisited that name on the old case files the night before no longer seemed by chance. "I do. She admitted to making advances towards Frank and was so stricken with guilt that she visited Jennifer and told her about it."

"Right. As I understand it, Alice worked with Missy Tucker a few years back. It was a small job, just manning a register at a local boutique shop that closed almost as quickly as it opened up."

"How long ago was this?"

"Maybe four years ago, give or take. The place was only open for like a year and a half. Everything in there was just too damned expensive."

"Have you reached out to Jennifer since Jack Tucker's murder?" Kate asked. "I imagine it brought a lot of new stuff up. New pain and questions."

"No. I thought about it. But I didn't want to assume that the Tucker murder would automatically bring up Frank's murder in her head. She may not even be aware of the way in which Jack was killed. She sort of clammed up after Frank died. We don't really talk much. Her entire life is completely centered around her children now. Well, that and community projects. She's very…*intimidating.* A lot of people see her as the poor widow, you know? But she's very involved. Community projects, school stuff for the kids. I think she's really active with the PTA."

"They had two, right?"

"Yes. Carter and Elisa. Jennifer *has* managed to sort of pick up the pieces…starting a new life and all that. But you know…I hate to throw her under the bus but even though she's a bit older now, she hangs around with younger ladies. I think it's because of the PTA at the middle school. There's a tight-knit group of ladies involved in the middle school PTA."

"How's that throwing her under the bus?" DeMarco asked.

"It's a small town, dear," Cass said. "People gossip all the time, especially the women. Maybe even more so with the women on the PTA. I know it might sound fickle, but that's Ashton for you. If there were rumors or gossip or anything related to Jack Tucker or the brief little working relationship between Missy Tucker and Alice Delgado, I guarantee you it was circulated in that little group."

"Are you not part of the group?" Kate asked. She took a huge bite of her cinnamon roll as she waited for an answer.

"Oh, I'm too old. I only know these women because you get to know everyone in a town like this."

Kate finished up her cinnamon roll, starting to get a good idea of where they'd have to go next. It would be yet another step back into her past but that was okay; if this visit with Cass Nobilini had turned out smooth, she figured anything was possible. Still, she felt a sense of foreboding as she thought about digging those old skeletons up, picking at those old scabs. It was also surreal to sense that in order to dig up any leads on her current case, she was going to have to keep revisiting an old one—an old one that had managed to escape her and taunt her for years afterward.

"Agent Wise, are you okay?"

Kate blinked, the sound of her name coming from Cass Nobilini jarring her out of her train of thought. "Yeah…I was just lost in my own thoughts for a second."

"Were you?" Cass asked, as if she understood perfectly. "Or were you—like me—stuck on trying to figure out how to escape that one certain part of your life you wish you could go back and change?"

To that, Kate could say nothing. It was as if the old lady had crawled into her mind and starting moving things around.

Would that be so bad? Kate wondered. *While she's in there, she can have these memories from her son's case and take them with her. I sure as hell don't want them anymore.*

But that wasn't exactly true. Because the longer she sat in Cass's kitchen, the more certain she became that crumbs from that old case would be what it took to close the Jack Tucker case.

CHAPTER EIGHT

It took quite a while for Kate and DeMarco to track down Alice Delgado. When they found that she was not at home, they requested her number from the bureau. The number went straight to voicemail. Kate then called the head office of the school that her son, Patrick, attended to see if they had any secondary contact information on file, since, like Jennifer Nobilini, Alice was actively involved with the PTA. That's where they hit pay dirt. The secondary information was not necessary, as Alice was currently at the elementary school, speaking with a local DJ about the set-up and playlist for the upcoming Fall Festival.

Kate and DeMarco entered the school, heading for the office first in order to be properly buzzed in. It was alarming to Kate to see that schools these days had to be so security-based. It had been twelve years since she had stepped foot in a school, and that had been to attend Melissa's graduation. While she had heard about some of the security measures taking place at even the smallest rural schools, seeing it firsthand was something very different—especially within an elementary school.

They found the gymnasium with no problem, following the sound of a few skidding sneakers and a bouncing basketball. When they got there, they saw some kids playing a game of five-on-five. On the right side of the gym, a gym teacher or coach of some sort watched the game. At the far end of the gym, a middle-aged woman was speaking to a tall man who seemed to be very interested in a particular corner of the gym. Kate assumed this to be the DJ that Alice was working with.

They walked to the far end, toward the DJ and the woman Kate assumed to be Alice. While she did not remember Alice Delgado nearly as well as Cass Nobilini, she assumed she would recognize the woman's face. She saw each and every face from that case at least once or twice a month in her head. It had gotten better over the years, but those faces and their expressions always seemed to find a way to come back to haunt her.

As they got closer, she saw that it was indeed Alice Delgado. She was still quite pretty, a woman having just crossed the border of thirty that could easily pass as twenty-one with a little extra time in front of the mirror. And as Alice's face came into view, Kate started

44

to recall how unpleasant the woman had been. Once she'd confessed to her attempt at seducing Frank Nobilini, she'd been honest and genuine in her remorse, but the guilt that had swept down on her had also turned her into something of a bitch. During follow-up visits and conversations, Alice had been confrontational and very heard to speak to.

The look Alice gave her when she noticed the two agents coming across the gym made Kate think that not only did Alice remember her quite well, but that she still held a grudge. Kate was reminded of Melissa who, on a few occasions, had referred to her own angry expressions as RBF, or "resting bitch face." And that's exactly what Kate was getting from Alice as she and DeMarco approached her.

"Ms. Delgado, can we have a minute of your time?" Kate asked.

Alice looked surprised, completely off of her game, but did her best to hide it with that stern and bitter look of anger.

"I'm in the middle of something," Alice said. But already, there was curiosity in her tone. In her eyes, too. Her disappointment and anger was quickly being overruled with her need to know why an FBI agent she met eight years ago had suddenly reappeared in the elementary school her seven year-old son was attending.

"I understand," Kate said. "But this will only take a moment and it's rather time sensitive."

She sighed, placed her hands on her hips, and looked to the DJ. "Could you give us a second?" she asked.

He nodded and walked away, heading over to check out the game of five-on-five. When he was safely out of earshot, Alice Delgado started speaking before Kate or DeMarco ever had the chance.

"Yes, I know about Jack Tucker. And I know that his murder was basically the same as Frank Nobilini's."

"Well, we're still lacking any sort of clues," Kate said.

"Just like last time, then?"

It was a biting remark. Kate was thrown off her game for a moment but was equally surprised when DeMarco took a single step forward and stood up for her. "No, not like last time. There are others dealing with their own grief right now. A woman named Missy Tucker—a woman we understand you worked with for a short time. So unless you wish what happened to Cass and Jennifer Nobilini eight years ago onto another widow, we'd appreciate your cooperation."

The look on Alice's face was one of utter disbelief. DeMarco might as well have just reached out and slapped her.

"Yes," Alice said, slowly starting to check her attitude. "We worked together for a small amount of time. The two of us and one other woman ran a little shop in town for a while."

"Did you get to know her well?" Kate asked.

"Fairly well, I'd say. We never really became close friends or anything like that, but we chatted quite a bit." She paused here and then added: "I'm sorry, but how does learning about Missy help you to find Jack Tucker's killer?"

"Because it's good to know if there was ever anything that came up in casual conversation that might have seemed odd to you," Kate said. "Anything that might have marred your opinion of their marriage."

Alice chuckled at this, shaking her head. "No. Good grief, they were like the picture of a perfect marriage. He was always doing things for her, always doting over her and the kids. I got pregnant very shortly after the FBI ditched Frank Nobilini's case. Married the father. And honestly, we always looked at the Tuckers' marriage as something to shoot for."

"Would it surprise you to know that Jack's mother was not the biggest fan of Missy?"

"It would not. That woman has issues. From what I understand, Jack was very close with his mother. This is just my own theory, but I think she took it as a competition when Jack got married and all of his attention went to his bride and their children. Shit...I knew that back when I first started working as a nanny in Ashton. Word gets around, you know. Apparently, Jack's mother was competitive...wanted her little boy under her thumb at all times."

It was clear that Alice was still a little uncertain about talking to them. Like Kate, it was clear that she had issues from the case eight years before that she had not quite resolved yet. Maybe the guilt or the hurt of confessing to Jennifer Nobilini. Kate started to feel bad for her in that moment. More than that, she started to feel guilty all over again for having never found Frank Nobilini's killer.

"We spoke with Cass Nobilini this morning," Kate said. "She indicated that a lot of mothers of school-age kids might be part of social circles that tend to hear things other people might not be privy to."

"You mean gossip?" Alice asked.

Kate said nothing, hoping her silence would speak for itself.

"You're not wrong," Alice said with a hint of annoyance. "But I stand by what I said. There was absolutely nothing to say about

46

Jack and Missy Tucker. They were perfect. Some of my friends sometimes use him as measuring stick—how they wish their husbands would love on them the way Jack loved on Missy. Let's face it, Agent Wise. Back in the day, when you and I first met, I was attracted to Frank Nobilini for a reason. I made a fool of myself for a reason. He was a good man, just like Jack. A kind and generous man and who was attractive as hell to me. It's attractive as hell to a lot of women, you know?"

"Any chance the Tuckers might have been just posturing it all?" DeMarco asked.

"If they were, they should be actors. In a town like Ashton, if you can somehow stay out of the grapevine, you're doing something right. So, no...the Tuckers were solid. If they were hiding secrets, they were pros about it."

"How about friends?" Kate asked. "While you were working with Missy, did she tend to talk about certain women that she hung out with?"

"Missy has one very good friend, a woman named Kelly Osman. There's another woman they tend to hang out with but I don't know her well. Jasmine Brooks is her name. They'd know a lot more about Missy and her life than I do. They're on the PTA as well, but they have kids in middle school. And that's the PTA Missy spends most of her time on. They tend to need the most help."

"Cass tells us that Jennifer Nobilini also serves with the PTA. Is that right?"

"Yes. She's pretty active, especially with art-related things. She sort of hops back and forth between this school and the middle school. She'll sort of poke her head into our little PTA circle of friends, but I think the gossip and small talk bothers her sometimes. She's extremely helpful with all things PTA but when the meetings and functions end, she mostly sticks to herself. Even when she helps out with her little community projects around town, she keeps a low profile. Doesn't want the attention, and keeps to herself."

"Are things...awkward between the two of you after what happened?"

Alice shrugged. "Maybe a bit. We don't really talk, you know? Even when we *are* in the same PTA meetings, we don't force it. We don't pretend nothing happened, but we're not hateful to one another, either. I have nothing against her. If anything, I respect the hell out of her."

"Thanks for the information," Kate said. "We'll let you get back to your project."

"Agent Wise...I think I speak on behalf of Cass Nobilini and Missy Tucker when I say that I hope you find the sonofabitch this time. Why come back and do this to someone else eight years later?"

"We're doing our best," Kate said.

A lopsided frown crossed Alice's face as Kate and DeMarco turned away. It was a frown that seemed to mock, to say: *Are you really?*

DeMarco fell in close to Kate as they exited the gymnasium. "Don't do that," she said.

"Don't do what?" Kate asked.

"Beat yourself up about the past. Leave the past where it is. You keep looking behind you and the present is going to sneak up on you and kick you in the teeth."

Kate nodded but in her head, she couldn't help but think: *I'm afraid it already has.*

***

Kelly Osman was not nearly as difficult to find as Alice Delgado had been. Kelly worked at a bed and breakfast in Ashton, a business she and her husband owned and operated. It was tucked away in the far end of town where the sparkle of the Hudson River could just barely be seen from the expansive side lawn. When Kate and DeMarco arrived at the Ashton Views Bed and Breakfast, Kelly Osman was outside, tending to the rather gorgeous flower garden. After the slight shock of the sudden appearance of a pair of FBI agents, Kelly led them to a nearby sitting area on the other side of the flower garden. A few butterflies flitted back and forth among several hydrangeas as Kate and DeMarco sat on a bench. Looking quite uncomfortable, Kelly took a seat in a lazy Adirondack chair.

"I spoke with Missy this morning," Kelly said as she continued to gauge the agents. "And I was at her house yesterday, just being there for her and delivering a casserole. I can't...God, I can't even start to figure out how to support her in this. She loved Jack so much..."

"That's one of the things we wanted to talk to you about," Kate said. "As her friend, I understand that it might be hard to think of such things, but we need you to think about anything from their past that might have put a crack in what seemed like their perfect marriage."

"You're looking for motive for someone to kill him, right?" She trailed off here, looking out in the direction of the Hudson

48

River. "You can look all you want, but I don't think you're going to find much of anything. If Jack had *any* enemies, it might have been from his work. He was an accountant. A big shot. You know that, right? He had some really big-name clients, too. From what I understand, he was like a savant at it. He was that kind of guy. Good at everything he touched. And Missy was always very quick to let everyone know it."

"She never said a cross word about him?" DeMarco asked.

"Not one that I ever heard. *Maybe* one time she griped about how he had a bad habit of always leaving his shoes by the coffee table, but that's about it."

"Did you know any of Jack's friends?" Kate asked.

"Well, he had a close-knit little group at the yacht club…"

"Yes, we've already spoken to them."

"You know…while I don't think I'd call them *friends*, my husband knew Jack pretty well at one point. A few years back, they'd meet with some of Jack's accounting associates and play a few rounds of tennis. And they also always attended what my husband called Dude Group—a group of dads that met maybe twice a year to smoke cigars and come up with plans to raise money for the schools. Fundraising and all that. The PTA without being the PTA."

"Do you think your husband would be willing to speak with us?" Kate asked.

"Sure. He's right inside, helping the cleaning crew. One second."

Kelly got up and ran into the two-story bed and breakfast. When she was gone, Kate sighed and rested her head against the back of the bench. "It was like this last time, too. There was never anything out of sorts or messed up about Frank Nobilini or his family. Not a single thing. No shady pasts, no real enemies to speak of. Just kind, everyday people with good lives."

"Maybe that's the connection right there," DeMarco suggested. Clean living, good lives. Success, maybe? Good marriages?"

"I don't know. Thinking back to that original case, with the Nobilinis…something about the way he was in the fetal position, his brains all over the wall. I always wondered if the killer was trying to tell us something…to almost make fun of them somehow."

They both dwelled on this as Kelly came back out of the bed and breakfast. Her husband walked behind her, a tall African-American man with plain good looks. He joined them in the sitting area, taking up another Adirondack by his wife.

"Lamont Osman," he said, extending his hand and shaking Kate's and then DeMarco's. "Kelly says you want to ask me some questions about Jack Tucker?"

"Yes. How close were you, exactly?"

"Not very. I mean, it was more than just a nod-and-wave sort of thing as of late, but we hung out here and there several years ago. The most time I ever spent with him was playing tennis a few years back. But when he made that job transition, that sort of dried up."

"And he never said or did anything that made you think that maybe the perfect life scenario was a ruse?"

"Nothing jumps out at me," he said. "But then again, it's different with men. We don't exactly get together and dish out gossip." He playfully nudged Kelly as he said this.

"Hey," she said, though there wasn't much defensiveness to it.

"Any gossip about the Tuckers you'd care to share?" DeMarco asked, lightly prodding.

"Nothing worth mentioning," Kelly said. "Whenever Jack's name came up, it was to compare with someone else's husband. Honestly, I think a few ladies in the Ashton circles had a little crush on him."

Just like with Frank Nobilini, Kate thought.

"Would anyone act on such a thing around here?" Kate asked.

"Doubtful. And even if a woman had the audacity to act on something like that, it's pretty well known that Jack Tucker isn't that sort of guy."

"We keep hearing that," Kate said. "How can you be so sure?"

"I know it sounds mean," Lamont said, "but Jack wasn't a very exciting dude. Yes, he was kind and yes, he was the sort to keep a clean nose and stay out of trouble. But because of all of that, he would sort of fade into the background, you know? The type of guy that, if he went to a party, you'd have to think really hard the next day about whether you saw him there or not. A good guy for sure but…well, if I'm being honest, sort of boring."

Boring, Kate thought. *There's that word again.*

Kate wracked her brain, trying to think of what else to ask, but she knew she'd end up coming to the same conclusion. That Jack Tucker was a nice guy, a real sweetheart, but sort of drab and plain.

Boring.

And then it dawned on her that maybe being boring, in and of itself, could potentially be a front for something else. And if a man could become very good at appearing boring, there was no telling what sorts of things he might become capable of hiding.

CHAPTER NINE

The day went by far too quickly as far as Kate was concerned. They'd gone from house to house—from family member to acquaintance and back again—and Kate felt that they had still gotten nowhere. It was the sort of case where she was practically just waiting for another body to show up. And God help her, she almost wanted that. It would at least present them with another opportunity to find evidence or clues.

They even revisited the alleyway where Jack Tucker's body had been discovered. Of course, they turned up nothing. Kate hadn't been expecting anything anyway—just hoping that maybe revisiting the scene would help her to view the murder through the eyes of the killer, to find some link between the alley and Ashton, the alley and Jack Tucker himself.

Following that, they huddled up back at the hotel, looking over the Jack Tucker case files. Kate made a meticulous list of things that they could potentially do to find some break in the case, prepared to pull an all-nighter if she had to. The list included: *examine shell casing from Ruger, speak to Detective Pritchard about how police handled scene from the start, check guest-logs of hotel Jack Tucker was staying in,* and *research client Jack was working for, RE: Adler and Johnson.*

Looking over the list, Kate knew that all of it was reaching. She could only hope that some useful nugget was buried in there somewhere.

She and DeMarco went their separate ways at 6:30. They agreed to split the list and reach out to bureau resources to get started on compiling the information. The first request Kate made was to find out recent clients and big-name jobs that Adler and Johnson had worked with. She was well aware that such a request could take several days and that she'd likely end up speaking with Daiju Hiroto tomorrow. She figured she could do some basic research online to get news-worthy details that were probably not relevant to their case but might lead them in the right direction. She planned to order dinner, shower, and do just that but was stopped before she could get into any of it when her cell phone rang.

51

She was rather confused and a bit hopeful when she saw that it was Duran. Maybe they'd had a break in DC. Maybe she could get out of New York and never have to step foot in Ashton again.

"Hello, Director Duran," she answered.

"Kate…I just got notified of a request you made for the last two years of clients working with Adler and Johnson. Can you tell me what that's about?"

"Well, I know for a fact that they are currently working for a client that works in the nuclear decommissioning industry. The world *nuclear* makes it easy to believe that maybe not everyone is a fan of such a company, no matter what their motives are. I thought it might be worth looking into the business practices and recent contract Adler and Johnson have drawn up. Maybe there was someone Jack Tucker worked with that had it in for him."

"You know how miserable that task is going to be. An accounting firm as big as Adler and Johnson is going to throw roadblocks at us every step of the way. It would be months—hell, even maybe years—before we got what we wanted. If we got it at all."

"I'm aware of that, sir. But we're running out of places to look."

"I'm starting to see that," Duran said. "And look, Kate, you understand that with your lack of results on the Nobilini case, it makes me wonder if I made a mistake sending you out there. I think I'm going to call you in. DeMarco, too."

"Sir, it's only been two days."

"You're right. but word is starting to spread around here that Jack Tucker was at one time working independently with a senator up there in New York, as a private accountant of sorts. He's worried about his own ass, but won't tell us why. Use your imagination there. Fraud, maybe. Something else unsavory…who knows? But he's getting antsy that this hasn't been wrapped yet and because of that, the bureau is under a spotlight."

"I'm hoping you're not going where it *sounds like* you're going with this," Kate said.

"You failed to close the Nobilini case eight years ago. If this story becomes a news item and your name pops up, people are going to make that connection. Yes, it would look bad for the FBI, sending an agent that already failed a similar—probably a *linked*—case. But it would not reflect well on you, either."

"So you're wanting to pull me to protect me?" Kate asked, her voice laced with sarcasm.

"View it how you want," Duran said. And the hell of it was, she did think she could hear some sorrow or disappointment in his voice. "But I want you back in DC by tomorrow morning. I'm going to line up someone else for this—someone that can view the case with fresh eyes."

"Someone younger?"

The question was out of her mouth before she could stop it, and she instantly regretted it.

Duran was silent for a while—for such a lengthy moment that Kate thought he had hung up on her. "View it how you'd like, Agent Wise. But I'm more concerned about your failure to wrap the case eight years ago and how another potential failure could look. Perhaps this is my fault. I should have thought about all of this before assuming you'd be the best fit."

"Well, you know what they say about assuming, sir."

"Agent Wise, I understand that the working relationship between you and I—and the bureau, as well, for that matter—is a special and strange one at this juncture. But I'd advise you to keep a civil tongue with me from now on."

This time, he *did* end the call. Kate could hear the audible click when he hung up. She tossed her phone on the bed and looked around the room, not sure if she wanted to be angry or saddened.

When she realized that she had to break this sudden news to DeMarco, she was able to finally decide on an emotion. As she slowly made her way out of the room and across the hall to her partner's room, frustration sank in like a lead weight. And by the time she knocked on DeMarco's door, it was closer to devastation.

CHAPTER TEN

When she walked through the front door of her house in Richmond eleven hours later, Kate could still feel the weight of the case—of the unsolved murders of both Frank Nobilini and Jack Tucker—as if it had been bolted to her shoulders. She carelessly dropped her single packed bag to the floor outside of the kitchen and went to the couch where she collapsed in a heap. She was pissed off but there was also a logical part of her that understood Duran's decision—and that he also had no damned business assigning her to the case in the first place if he was going to be worried about covering the bureau's ass.

To get her mind off of it, she stretched out on the couch and texted Melissa. **Back home. Dead-end case. How are you and the little one?**

She then pulled her personal laptop off of the coffee table and opened up her email. She sent a short and sweet email to Duran, copying in DeMarco, just to let him know that she was back home and officially off of the case. It took a lot of effort not to throw in a little jab of some sort, but she managed.

She wondered if maybe Melissa would be able to come over with Michelle later, maybe for dinner. Or if Melissa was busy (she did, after all, have a family and a life of her own), maybe Allen would want to come over.

She'd be happy with either one, so long as she didn't have to spend the afternoon alone. If she did that, she knew her mind would stay stuck on the Jack Tucker case, trying to figure it out and dig for any sort of clues until her eyes slapped shut on her later in the night. As she managed to pull herself from the couch to see what she had in the fridge for lunch, her cell phone dinged at her as Melissa responded.

Sorry for the dead end. Michelle and I are good.

She responded with: **Want to join me for dinner later?**

The response came back quickly, making Kate assume that Melissa was on a break at work. **Sorry. No can do. Family dinner tonight. It's a big deal to the hubs.**

She was disappointed, sure. But she understood. Frankly, she was happy and relieved that Melissa had managed to become part of a happy and well-managed family. With a sad smile, she sent her daughter: **Maybe tomorrow we can do breakfast?**

She received a **Probably not** within seconds. **I have work. And then we're leaving town for a few days to go see Terry's parents. Sorry, mom. But I'm glad you're back home and safe.**

She completely understood it all but still, it hurt. She wondered if this was how Melissa had felt all those times she'd needed her mother but her mother was occupied with work. She thought of little Michelle and although she had seen her less than two weeks ago, she couldn't help but feel as if she were being an absentee grandmother. Even when she *was* home and not being occupied with her job with bureau, her mind was always there. Wanting to get better, wanting to stay sharp, wanting to make sure her age did not define her.

She set her phone down and then set about making lunch. She did her best to tuck the text conversation with Melissa into the back of her head.

She stood there, staring into the refrigerator, feeling lost. *On the hunt for a killer one day and realizing that I badly need to clean out my fridge the next,* Kate thought. *What the hell kind of a life is this?*

As she settled down at the kitchen table with a tuna sandwich, she couldn't help but wonder if Duran had a point yesterday in his thinly veiled little barbs. After all, she had retired a year and a half ago because she felt that she deserved it—that she had given all she could and that she had left her best years in the bureau behind her. Maybe she should have left it that way. If she had, she wouldn't currently be eating a cold tuna sandwich by herself, wondering if Duran, DeMarco, Michelle, Allen, and God only knew who else saw her as nothing more than a sad aging lady who just couldn't let go of her glory years.

Maybe this was her sign. Maybe this was the final indicator she needed to show once and for all that it was over. She should have stayed retired. She *should* retire. For good. Duran would probably see it as a godsend—an easy way out of a situation he likely wished he had never created.

She looked to her phone. All it would take was a single call. She didn't think Duran would put up too much of a fight. If he put one up at all.

She grabbed the phone and thought about it. She saw the body of Jack Tucker in the alley and then the body of Frank Nobilini in a very similar alley. Both shot in the back of the head as if it were nothing.

The shell casings from the Ruger.

Execution style.

Two relatively plain and boring men, discarded as if they were nothing.

Boring...

She had no idea why that word seemed so important to her. It continued to nag at her, seeming to itch along the back of her head.

She pulled up her contacts and instead of calling up Duran to bail out of their little arrangement, she called Allen. He answered right away but he seemed to be lacking his usual good cheer.

"Hey there, Katie."

She smiled. She'd hated that name as a kid but she loved it when Allen used it. It made her feel young. She assumed it made *him* feel young as well.

"You got plans tonight?" she asked.

"I thought you were in New York."

"Yeah, that was fleeting. A dead-end case that, quite frankly, has me feeling a little down. I thought you might like to come over and change that."

"Yeah...I don't know, Kate."

There was caution in his voice, as if he were choosing his words very carefully.

"Everything okay?" she asked.

"I'd like to think so, but I don't know. Kate...I know I mentioned this once before and we just sort of shrugged it off but I'm not a fan of only being called on or needed when it's convenient for you. When the job comes calling, it's Kate on Duty. You're in this whole other world. But then when things are in a lull, you rely on me. Honestly, I don't really care and if we were twenty-five years younger, I wouldn't care at all. But...I don't know."

"That feels a little unfair."

"Oh, I know. And I hate to even mention it. But it's unfair to me, too. You have to see that, right?"

She figured he had a point. She felt a little self-involved not to have realized it before. "So what do we do?"

"For starters, I'm going to stay here tonight. I think it might do me some good to not come running at your beck and call."

"Allen, I never meant for it to sound like that."

"I know that, too. And that's why I think maybe we cool it for a while. Take some time, Kate. Figure out what it is you really want. When you think you have an actual answer, please do call me. Because I'll be honest with you...I think I was starting to fall pretty hard."

56

"Yeah, me too." A flush of heat raced through her as she admitted this to him.

"Let's check back in later. As selfish as it might sound, I don't think I'm emotionally prepared to be second to work...especially in a new relationship. Especially at this age."

"Allen...I can't..."

He gave her a moment and then asked: "You can't what?"

But she wasn't sure how to respond. How should she explain the sense of failure and worthlessness she was feeling? How could she explain the feeling of being haunted by a case—by two men who had been killed in the same way, their killer eluding her completely?

"I can't make that decision right now," she said. She hated the feeling of the words in her mouth but knew that they were absolutely true.

"It's okay. I'm serious. Let's check back in later. You reach out to me when you're ready. I'll be here, though I can't promise for how long." He paused, cleared his throat to shove aside the emotion that was trying to climb into his voice, and then ended the conversation with a simple "Bye."

He ended the call, leaving Kate with a dead line in her hand. The feeling that swept through her was far too similar to what she had felt when Duran had ended their call yesterday. Disappointment. Sadness. The feeling of not being good enough.

As much as she loathed doing it, she felt herself starting to cry. First, realizing that she was slowly starting to drift away from Melissa, and now Allen had apparently had enough. Jesus, was she really *that* divided when it came to her personal life and her new situation within the bureau? Rogue tears cascaded down her cheeks. In that moment, her world felt entirely empty and void. Just her and a stupid tuna sandwich.

And somewhere out there, a killer who had shot two men in the back of the head, execution style.

***

When her phone rang just after six that afternoon, she was hoping it would be Melissa. She was almost equally as pleased to find that it was not her daughter, but DeMarco.

"You feeling like a total fuck-up today, too?" DeMarco asked her.

"A bit. But you shouldn't. I think you were removed just because you were paired with me. If anything, I think I need to offer you an apology."

"Don't you dare," DeMarco said with a laugh. "You probably can't tell because of my cool and icy demeanor, but I've learned a lot from you. I was excited when they paired me with you seven months ago and I'm still excited. I'm just as frustrated as you about being pulled from the case, though."

Kate thought about venting to her about the call she'd had with Allen earlier in the day but decided against it. Yes, they needed to become closer to one another, but that didn't necessarily mean they needed to fill any down time or silence with relationship grievances.

"Any idea what Duran is going to assign you to now that you're off of the Jack Tucker case?"

"I don't know yet. I'm going to make a push to dig into the Adler and Johnson stuff you were requesting. I'm sure it'll be better than whatever surveillance detail he'll stick me on until something better comes along."

"You don't have to do that."

"I want to. A well-to-do man working with people who are *that* filthy rich and connected to nuclear decommissioning...I don't know. It sounds rife with possible scenarios."

Kate thought so, too. But she also knew that Duran had been right yesterday. Pulling those kinds of details would take months, and they'd be bogged down in paperwork and legalities the entire time.

"Well, let me know when you have a free weekend. I'd love to have you down here for a day out on the town."

"Include that cute grandbaby of yours in the deal, and I'll see what I can do. Later, Kate."

Kate ended the call, warmed by the gesture DeMarco had made by calling. It was a little unlike her and, Kate thought, was probably an attempt at putting the final touches on their attempt at patching up the tension that had been between them for most of their visit to New York.

It was even more depressing to realize that she had somehow managed to grow more attached to DeMarco, a representation of work, than she had with her family and personal life over the last half a year or so.

Then just quit, she thought. *The FBI will be just fine without you. Do you really think that highly of yourself?*

Again, she knew it would be easy. Just one phone call. But she knew she couldn't. Especially right now. If it had come on the heels of a successfully closed case, that would be one thing. But to quit now, right after yet another case in Ashton had managed to slip through her hands, it would be too much like admitting defeat—too much like giving up.

Feeling somewhere between melancholy and defeated, Kate changed into pajamas and sat idly in front of the television with a cup of decaf coffee. She stared at the television screen, tuned to one of those generic HTV home and garden shows, but she was not truly watching it. Her mind was elsewhere, as was usually the case.

Her mind wandered, running around the mental maze that was the Jack Tucker case as if she were stuck in some weird hedge maze. And before she could allow herself to get trapped in it, she cut the TV off and went upstairs into the guest bedroom. There, she walked into the closet and opened the door in the back, the only entryway into the house's attic. She climbed the wooden stairs and entered the attic, a space that was always at least ten to fifteen degrees cooler than the rest of the house.

She turned on the light—a simple overhead bulb without a casing or shield. She and Michael had always planned on finishing the space off but had kept delaying it, waiting until they had more than enough money so they could make it really nice space. But after Michael died, she forgot all about it, not even thinking about finishing it until the random and rare moments she found herself walking into the space. The floor was solid, though it was nothing more than overlapped sheets of plywood that had been nailed into the underlying beams. She walked across this thin excuse for a floor toward an old beaten and worn miniature filing cabinet that she had shoved in the far corner many years ago.

There was also an old lawn chair propped against it, for use on the few times she had come up here. She unfolded it and sat down in it as she opened up the top of the three drawers of the cabinet. Inside, there were a few old folders and albums—all related to work. There were newspaper clippings of cases she had knocked out of the park, old awards and certificates for her successes, copies of closed cases she had used for reference materials, and on and on.

She skipped to the section she knew she was looking for: her handwritten and printed out personal notes on the Frank Nobilini case. They were paperclipped to Xeroxed copies of the actual case files, along with the handful of police reports she had accumulated regarding people in Ashton.

She had poured over these notes for more nights than she cared to admit. As she took the notes out and started to read them, a vibrant memory of Michael coming into the attic just after midnight popped into her head.

"We have a king-sized bed," he had said. *"It gets awful big when you're not in it."*

"Sorry," she had said, putting the folders back.

"It's okay," he said. *"I know that I'm but a second fiddle to your work."* He'd smiled here and then kissed her lightly on the back of the neck. *"But if you come to bed with me right now, I promise to make it worth your while."*

He had taken her hand and pulled her up out of the seat...

She grew a little teary-eyed at that. That memory was a fresh one—maybe three years before he had died. It was so fresh that she could nearly feel his breath on her neck.

"I'm sorry, Michael," she said.

And with that, she turned her full attention to the files in her hands. And this time, without anyone to come pull her away, she fell completely into them.

CHAPTER ELEVEN

She had the dream again.

Frank Nobilini had been walking toward her, stepping in the blood that had seeped out of the bathroom. Only this time, instead of his wife following after him, he was accompanied by Jack Tucker. They both held handguns, offering them to her.

"Here," Frank said. "Do it. Shoot us. Kill us. It's just the same as not finding who put these holes in the back of our heads."

He turned to show her the hole he was referencing. Jack did the same. As they turned their backs to her, the holes in the backs of their heads started to grow in size, eating away the rest of the heads like some strange fungus.

Kate sat up with a start, her heart surging in her chest. She felt her stomach lurching at that last image from the dream and for a moment, she thought she might need to rush to the bathroom to throw up. But she took a moment to steady her breathing and managed to fight the urge away.

She felt a little out of sorts as she readied herself for the day. By seven, she had the coffee brewing and some soft '70s rock playing on Spotify. She dressed for the day and ate breakfast at the kitchen bar. If not for the music playing, the house would have felt very much like a crypt or tomb. She'd been alone in this house a considerable amount of time ever since Michael died and Melissa had moved out but now, knowing that Allen wanted a break and that Melissa seemed too busy to spend time with her, it made it feel like some remote, ancient land where she was stranded and alone.

She needed to get out. She needed to get away from this unhealthy tension. She needed to work off her frustration, nerves, and feeling of loss. She wondered if she could call someone at the gym to have someone to spar with later today. A few rounds in the ring would certainly do her a world of good.

And while that was indeed a promising thought, another thought came to mind right behind it. Even the mere thought if it made her heart lighten a bit. She thought of a place that had felt like home ever since her first year with the bureau, a place that, whether it was sacrilegious or not, had nearly felt like a church experience to her when her career and life had seemed out of sorts.

Kate finished up her breakfast, went to the closet to grab her sidearm, and headed for the firing range.

***

While she would much prefer the more aesthetically pleasing shooting range at the bureau in Washington, there was something to be said for a locally owned shooting range. The people who owned and operated it—as well as the people who paid money to use the range—were not there because of training or necessity. No, they visited the range for the love of the sport, for their appreciation of firearms. Nearly every time she had been to her range of choice in Richmond—a place called Scope Skills, she had seen at least one person taking training courses for a conceal and carry permit.

As she walked through the entrance that morning, though, she was not at all surprised to see that she was the only one there. It was, after all, a little shy of ten o'clock on a Monday morning. She carried a bag in over her shoulder, containing her bureau-issued Glock 19M. She had no magazines on her, but she knew that Scope Skills carried the kind she needed.

She checked in at the front desk, where the owner, Jerry—a butch and well-rounded guy who could have been a stand-in for a WWE wrestler—greeted her with a smile.

"Agent Wise," he said. It was a running joke among them, as she had teased him before about how having a retired agent frequent your range meant that your range had better be following every law known to man with a scrupulous eye. He also thought it was awesome that a fifty-six-year-old woman rocked the gun range the way she did. "How's the morning treating you?"

"Not as well as I'd like," she said.

"Practicing for some big case or something?"

"Nah," Kate said. "Just letting off some steam."

"I hear that."

Kate booked a kiosk, purchased two magazines of ammo for her Glock, and then headed to the back. The smell of the place instantly calmed her. It was not necessarily the smell of expelled rounds that had somehow sunk into every corner and crack of the place. It was the smell of guns finely polished, of a slight tinge in the air that she liked to think was the expelled excitement and concentration of a shooter with a keen eye.

She loaded up the Glock, sent the first target out—a basic black-and-white representation of a human figure placed against a black background—and assumed a shooter's stance. She breathed in deeply, as if resetting herself, and felt her muscles settle into a groove.

She opened her eyes and fired. And fired again.

The next ten minutes were almost Zen-like for her. She'd always found this odd because at no point in her training had she ever truly become enamored with firearms. She knew the basics, plus enough to be able to participate in a mid-tier conversation about them, but she was far from what someone might describe as a "gun nut." She just knew that firing them at targets in a safe and secure environment was calming to her in the same way some people enjoyed fishing or baking. She wasn't the type of agent that could name each and every gun by simply looking at it, nor did she know much military weaponry history. She had always kept it fairly simple, using whatever the bureau's current issue was, with the exception of the Sig Sauer she had received as a gift from Agent Greene, her first partner.

She stopped firing suddenly, a thought dawning on her out of nowhere.

I've always used whatever the bureau has issued because I've been comfortable with it. I love this 19M because I am familiar with it and know it well. Before this, I felt comfortable with the standard-issue 9mm they sent some of us into the field with. I've always been comfortable with these more compact and easy-to-carry weapons because it's what I know.

She thought of the gun that had been sued to kill Frank Nobilini and Jack Tucker. She thought of the shell casings, identified pretty quickly by law enforcement as having come from a Ruger Hunter Mark IV.

The same gun on both men, eight years apart. Apparently, that's a gun the killer was comfortable with...

Kate cleaned up the little bit of mess at her station and left the kiosk. As she headed for the front of the building where Jerry was currently arranging his accessory counter, he gave her a strange look.

"You've got sixteen minutes left for what you paid," he said.

"I know. But I was wondering if you could maybe help me out with something. You're fairly knowledgeable on guns, right?"

"Sure. And by the way, I prefer fairly knowledgeable over some of the descriptors my wife chooses to use when it comes to me and guns."

"What do you know about the Ruger Hunter Mark IV?"

Jerry thought for a moment, his arms crossed over his massive chest. "Well, I know that I don't have one here. I've never fired one, actually. But I've seen some at gun shows and what-not. Some of them come with a threaded barrel for suppressors. I guess in your line of work, it would be a pretty good choice for someone wanting to stealthily take someone out. It's a rimfire pistol and I think the newer ones can be taken apart really quickly. It's because of a really cool takedown mechanism."

"Have you yourself ever had someone ask if you could get one in for them?"

"No. While it's not a specialty gun or particularly hard to find, it's also not very popular."

"So it's also not considered a standard enough gun to be used haphazardly by just about anyone wanting something to protect their homes, right?"

"No."

She thought about this for a minute, feeling a trail start to assemble itself in her head. "With the suppressor, it would make the shot a little cleaner, too, right?"

Jerry shrugged. "I'm not sure. Maybe, maybe not. It depends on the shooter and what they're shooting at. It's a sleek gun, though."

"It sounds like it would be a perfect choice for someone who might want to quietly kill someone and leave no trace, right?"

"Except for the shell casings, yes, I suppose. Why do you ask?"

"Because I'm starting to wonder what sort of person would be comfortable enough to use such a gun on a regular basis."

Jerry grinned uncomfortably here and leaned forward on the counter. "Yeah, I think it would be a pretty good choice for someone that needed to kill quickly and quietly. I'm pretty sure I remember reading something about it not too long ago, how there are some people rumored to be working with the mob that use weapons just like that. Or maybe it was one of my military-style documentaries that I'm always watching—which my wife *also* hates, by the way."

Kate knew exactly where she needed to go, what she needed to do. She started for the door quickly, the trail in her head now complete.

"Thanks, Jerry," she called on her way out. "This was a huge help!"

He said something to her, but she was already outside. Yes, she knew what the next step was, even though Duran would tar her a new one if he found out. Still, she had to...to keep herself sane and to feel like she had not given up.

There was a downside, though. Wasn't there always?

While she knew the step she needed to take, it was a backward one. Once again, she was going to have to take a big step back into her past. And while it was a step in the right direction, she couldn't help but feel that it seemed more like falling behind than moving forward.

CHAPTER TWELVE

Every now and then a potential lead would come to her and there would be some extra bit of information or convenience that would make her feel as if it was simply meant to be. She'd experienced it more times than she could count during her career as an agent and she felt it now, as she drove out of Richmond and toward the much smaller town of Dilwyn, Virginia. She had put away plenty of criminals in the course of her career, one hundred two to be exact, and they were scattered all over the US, in different prisons according to where they had committed their crimes in most cases.

But of those one hundred two criminals, there were a handful who had ended up in Buckingham Correctional Center. It was located in the center of Buckingham County, hidden away in a little nothing of a town called Dilwyn. Kate had visited the prison about five or six times in her career, so when she made the trip that morning it was like a little exodus back in time.

One of the men that she had taken down who ended up in Buckingham was a man named Alvin Carpenter. He had once worked out of the northeast coast as a hitman for hire. He'd had ties with the mob and an unnamed syndicate in New York. But when Kate had finally brought him down after the attempted murder of a bio-fuels engineer in 2005, he had been at work just outside of Alexandria, Virginia.

He had been silent on the names of his clients, never offering them up even in a plea bargain attempt during the trial. When two hits had been chained to him while he'd been in prison, his twenty-five years had been upgraded to a life sentence. Kate had not spoken to him since his initial arrest so she had no idea how he might react to seeing her. But she figured there was only one way to find out, and since she was no longer actively on the Jack Tucker case, she had plenty of time to spare.

She arrived at the Buckingham Correction Center just shy of 11:30, the drive vacant of traffic and taking less than an hour and a half. As she walked in, she tried to remember the last time she'd had to visit the place. She figured it had been at least ten years. She also wondered if she'd see any familiar faces and, if so, if they would recognize her own. The feeling of venturing back into her past had her looking for just about anything to latch on to, anything that might make her feel a little closer linked to that time in her career.

But as she walked into the lobby and to the visitors desk, she saw no familiar faces. In fact, she barely recognized the building at all. It had that stale yet almost astringent smell that had, weirdly enough, always reminded her of the way a post office smelled.

She checked in at the visitors desk, introduced herself, and made a request to speak with Alvin Carpenter. Because of her retirement and new agreement with the bureau, there were several hold-ups. As the woman at the check-in desk made a few calls, the weight of the situation fell on Kate. If they had to call the bureau, she'd be screwed. She had no idea how Duran would react to her still snooping into the case when he had, in so uncertain terms, removed her from it less than two days ago.

It took a while, but this worry was erased when, twenty-five minutes after making the request, she was given permission. Apparently, her name on the original arrest records of an inmate by the name of Alvin Carpenter had ended up being enough to grant her access to the prisoner.

Kate was escorted out of the lobby and down a connecting hallway that led to the prison itself. She was scanned by a walk-through metal detector and was finally assigned a guard to walk her to one of the visitation rooms.

"How has the inmate's behavior been these last few years?" Kate asked the guard as he led her to the visitation room.

"Not much out of him, really. He's quiet, stays to himself. He reads a lot. Lots of biographies and things like that. Not someone that really sticks out, you know?"

Kate remembered Carpenter being rather reserved. When he'd gotten his sentence, there had been no crying or wailing. He'd nodded in the courtroom and taken it like a man. She assumed that any hitman who would be willing to take the names of his clients to the grave even when several years of freedom were offered in exchange would be a resilient and almost resigned man once he was behind bars. He accepted life as it was, expecting nothing special. He'd killed people, now he was doing his time, and that was his life.

It made Kate feel like this might be a wasted trip. Would a man like that give her the kind of information she was looking for?

No use in trying to talk yourself out of it now, she thought as she was escorted into the visiting room. She took a seat at the small and battered conference table as the guard took position in the back of the room. He crossed his arms and stared at the door, apparently waiting for another guard to being in Alvin Carpenter. He then looked back at her, as if he was being extra protective. Maybe he felt uneasy with the idea of a woman her age meeting with a man like Alvin Carpenter.

The door opened a little over five minutes later. Carpenter came in first, his hands cuffed behind his back and a puzzled look on his face. He looked around the room for a moment, as if he didn't even see her. But when he finally realized what was happening, she saw the look of recognition and then the slight smile that crossed his face.

Alvin Carpenter was in his late fifties now. His head was shaved and he wore a mostly gray beard that was closely trimmed to his face. He had that same look of calm acceptance on his face that Kate remembered so clearly from the last time she had seen him at his final court hearing.

"Agent Wise," he said with something close to delight in his voice. "I'm not even lying when I say it's nice to see you. This is unexpected."

"Oh, it is for me, too," Kate said. "You look well."

He shrugged as he took the seat on the other side of the table. The guards both looked to Kate and she nodded. "We're good."

"We'll be outside the door if you need us," the guard that escorted her said. And with that, they exited the room.

"I do have to say," Alvin said, "I can't figure out why you'd visit me. You and your bureau friends found out everything—the other two jobs, all the details. I'd say I was pretty thoroughly buried."

"Well, I'm here for a different reason. And I hope you'll consider listening very closely and considering a request I have."

"I'm not giving up the names of my clients," he said.

"No, I know. I'm beyond that. This is different. Mr. Carpenter...if you had to take a guess, how many other people did you have in your network before you were arrested that were either hitmen or worked very closely with them?"

He thought about this for a moment before answering, waving his hand in a *so-so* motion. "Ten. Maybe a dozen. Of course, I have no way of knowing if they're all even still alive."

"Is there a weapon of choice among hitmen?" she asked. "Sure, you want to be quiet...that's a given. But was there a go-to gun that you ever preferred?"

"I toyed with sniper rifles for a while," Alvin said. "And I know it will make me sound like a monster, but I never cared for them because the target is so far away. For the job to be truly effective, I believe in being close and personal when that trigger is pulled." A slight grimace crossed his face, as if he were being unnerved by his own choice of words. "But I always went with a Beretta 70s."

"What about a Ruger? A Hunter Mark IV?"

He tilted his head and nodded. "A little heavy-handed for my tastes, but yes. That could go very well, so long as it was threaded for a silencer." He smiled again and sat forward, apparently very interested. "Are you chasing down another hitman, Agent Wise?"

"I don't know quite yet," she said. She also sat forward, letting him feel as if she were engaged—as if she was hanging on his every word. She hoped it might make him a little more willing to cough up some information.

"Ask what you need to," Carpenter said. "I must tell you, this is the most exciting thing that has happened to me in years. A break in the monotony. I greatly appreciate it."

"How would someone find you? I know many years have passed since I brought you in, so times have changed. But based on what you know, how might someone go about actually hiring a hitman today?"

"Many ways," he said. He then sat back, his posture relaxed. She knew that he was trying to figure out whether or not to go on with it. A man like Carpenter might fear that he was getting some colleagues from his past in trouble with this sort of information. "Can I ask why you're asking?" he said.

"I'm afraid not. And I know you're a man of integrity. That's why you never gave the names of the people that hired you. But I can give you my word that my current investigation has nothing to do with anyone you were ever involved with. Or, rather, if it is, it would only turn out to be a happy coincidence on the bureau's end."

That seemed to satisfy Carpenter. "Well," he said, "for someone that doesn't already have the contacts, the internet is going to be the place to start."

"The dark web, I assume?"

"Sure, there are plenty of guys for hire on there. Actually, guys in my profession just go where they need to go on the dark web and the jobs are there waiting for them. But even most people that want to hire hitmen aren't quite dumb enough to search around on the dark web. Instead, there are more public, more popular places. Craigslist, for example."

"How is that even possible?"

"The ads are worded very cleverly. Or, in some cases, if you go the personals, you'll find ads that are worded just oddly enough that it's clear that it's a hitman for hire or, in some cases, even people in search of a hitman. I see your look of disbelief, but it's more common than you think."

"I see..."

"Do you?" He paused here and sighed. "Tell me about the case and maybe I can point you in the right direction."

Now it was Kate's turn to be hesitant. She knew that even if Carpenter did decide to blab about it to his fellow inmates, the information would not leave these walls. But honestly, she didn't see him spreading it. Murderer or not, she did not think he was the sort of man who would use gossip or his knowledge of current FBI cases to his advantage while in jail—if such a thing was even possible.

So she told him about the Tucker case and how it appeared that it was directly related to the Frank Nobilini case. She told him about the weapon that had been used on both victims as well as the fact that both had appeared to have been execution-style shootings. Carpenter listened intently as she gave him the details. And before she was done, she could see a slight sense of understanding in his eyes.

"You say this is in New York?" he asked.

"Yes. Both bodies discovered in alleys in Midtown, but they were residents of Ashton. Why? Do you think you have something?"

"Probably not," he said with a shrug. "But the whole execution-style thing...that's a bit much. A power trip, really. You want to just get in there, get the job done, and split. Taking the time to get the jump on the guy and then making him get down on his knees...that's pure ego. Your killer is probably full of himself. Thinks a little too highly of himself. And I used to hear people talk about this one guy that worked up that way—in Queens and Manhattan, in particular. A real dick. Had a power trip for days. Clean work, good at what he did, but always taking one too many risks just to make himself stand out, you know?"

"You got a name?" she asked.

"I do, actually. But honestly, I doubt it's his real name. He was Zeus Beringer—I *think* that was his last name. The name Zeus seemed fitting because he went about his work like he thought he was a god, you know?"

"You think he lives in New York?"

"No clue. But I think that's where the bulk of his jobs were out of."

"Did you ever meet him?"

Carpenter gave her a wry smile and shrugged. "No clue. He wouldn't be much of a hitman if he told me his identity, now would he?"

Kate considered the information. It certainly seemed to line up with what she knew of both the Nobilini and the Tucker cases. It was the sort of information that, if she were still officially on the case, would certainly warrant the effort of locating this man known as Zeus Beringer.

"Thank you, Mr. Carpenter," she said, getting up from her seat.

"That's it?" he asked, disappointed. "Nothing else you need?"

She frowned, nearly feeling bad for him. This break in his monotony had been something out of the ordinary—something exciting, even. And now, less that twenty minutes after it had started, it was coming to an end.

"I'm afraid so," she said. "But I genuinely do thank you for your time."

He started to look irritated, but Kate turned away and headed for the door. The guard was already opening it for her when Carpenter called out from behind her.

"Agent Wise?"

"Yes?" she said, turning back around.

"While the man you're looking for is certainly a low-life asshole, you have to consider...there was someone out there that saw it fit to hire such a man. And in the end, isn't that person you need to be concerned about?"

Kate let the comment sink in as she walked through the doorway. By the time she returned to her car, it sat there like a heavy rock poised to fall off a cliff.

CHAPTER THIRTEEN

Kate didn't travel very far after leaving the prison. She drove ten miles down the road, stopped by a McDonald's for lunch, and then pulled over in the parking lot. While she ate a very dry and flavorless salad, she called up DeMarco. As the phone rang in her ear, it occurred to her that what she was about to ask could potentially get DeMarco in trouble. And as that reality sank in, she decided to hang up.

But before she could, DeMarco's voice was in her ear. "Agent Wise. How are you?"

"I'm…good."

A brief silence filled the line, broken by DeMarco's musical chuckle. "You're still working the case, aren't you?"

"Maybe."

"Find anything?"

"I think so. Not sure yet. I was hoping you could get me some information without tipping off Duran."

"Kate…are you sure?"

She called me Kate rather than Agent Wise, Kate thought. *It feels like I'm being scolded. And maybe she has a point.*

"You're right. I can't ask you to—"

"I don't mind," DeMarco interrupted. "I can get you whatever you want without Duran finding out. I'm just worried about the repercussions on your end if it comes to anything."

"I'll be fine," Kate said. "After all, it may be nothing."

DeMarco hesitated, considering the options. Finally, she said: "What do you need?"

***

It took DeMarco less than forty-five minutes to come up with a list of addresses for males with the last name Beringer in New York City. There were thirty-seven in all—with an additional one hundred eighteen when alternate spellings were included—but Kate narrowed them down to the areas of Queens and Manhattan. And while there was no listing for a *Zeus* Beringer, there was only one listing in them all where the middle initial was listed as a Z. This was Malcolm Z. Beringer, a resident of Queens.

Had she actively been on the case, this would have been fantastic news indeed. Even if the lead turned out to be nothing at all, it was at least a solid indicator that the work she had put in today had been effective.

She plugged the address into Google Maps and winced at what she saw. From her current spot in the McDonald's parking lot, it would take her nearly six and a half hours to drive to Queens. She'd made far longer drives in the past, but never one that would be driving directly against the orders of her director.

"What's he going to do?" she asked herself. "Fire me?"

Hearing those words out loud helped her a great deal. So what if he *did* fire her? It would at least make her decision of whether or not to continue pursuing this part-time position much easier. She also knew that the alternative was that she might actually help break the case. And while Duran would no doubt reprimand her in some way for going against his orders, it would be worth it.

Not just to find the killer, but to finally close a case that had been haunting her for nearly a decade.

That made the decision easy. The long drive really wasn't even that much of an inconvenience. Besides…she had nothing but time to spare.

What else was retirement for, if not long spontaneous drives across the country?

***

She was fortunate enough to get into the city just behind the afternoon rush of post-work traffic, the gridlocked hell that occurred between 5:00 and 6:30. Still, by the time she pulled up in front of Malcolm Z. Beringer's address, it was 7:02 and the drive had taken its toll. She was cramped and tired and a little cranky. She nearly got out of the car and headed straight for the door but thought better of it.

If that was indeed the address of a hitman or some other unsavory man, she had to cover her ass—particularly because she did not have the bureau's backing. She idly wondered if there were already other agents in the area to cover the case. She made a mental note to ask DeMarco about it the next time they spoke.

Thinking of DeMarco, she pulled out her cell phone and sent her a text. **I'm here. Wish me luck.**

She then got out of the car and walked to the building. She saw a control panel along the front of the door. It was the sort of apartment building where you had to be rung in by the person you were visiting. Again, though, she got lucky. There was a delivery driver for Vinny's Pizzeria walking up the stairs, carrying two pizzas toward the door. Kate bided her time, waited for him to announce himself over the intercom, and then hurried up behind him.

"Let me get that for you," she said, taking the door as it was buzzed. She opened it, allowing the delivery guy inside, and then fell in behind him.

"Thanks," he said.

"Thank *you,* " she replied.

She then took the stairs to the third floor, the address telling her that Malcolm Z. Beringer—whom she could not stop thinking of as Zeus thanks to Alvin Carpenter—lived in apartment 306. She walked to the apartment as if she belonged in the building, like she made the journey through the halls and stairways every day.

This act came to a stop as she reached apartment 306. She had a rough idea of how she wanted to initiate the conversation. But she also knew that a man with a history of any sort of murder—especially murder for hire—was always going to be on the lookout for bait-filled conversations…especially from strangers.

She knocked on the door and stepped back, making sure that anyone on the other side would clearly be able to see her through the peephole in the door. When there was no answer, she knocked again, louder this time. She even pressed her head to the door, curious to see if she could hear any movement from inside.

After thirty seconds, she was confident that no one was home. Or, if they were, they were dead asleep at 7:15 in the afternoon. She took a quick look up and down the hallway, found herself alone, and pulled the lock pick out of her coat pocket. She worked quickly, relishing the feel of something she had once done many times before. Now, years removed, it felt almost like a superpower. She felt and heard the lock turn all at once. Instinctually falling back on her training, she knew to enter at once. If there *was* anyone inside, they'd expect a bit of a pause between having their lock picked and the actual entrance. By going in right away, it created the element of surprise.

She entered at once, her hand instantly going for her Glock. She knew that any use of it would get her into serious trouble, as she was not actually on the case. Still, her need to survive was a bit stronger than anything else in that moment.

The door entered into a small kitchen. There were a few dirty dishes in the sink, and an empty pizza box sitting on the counter. The kitchen led directly into the living area. A lamp was on in the corner, dimly lighting the place. There was a single armchair in the center of the space with a TV and a bookshelf along the far wall. It wasn't a wreck of a place by any means, but it was clear that Zeus did not care much about interior decorating.

She stood in the center of the living area, now confident that no one was home. She ventured into the apartment's only bedroom and had a look around. There was nothing out of the ordinary at first glance. A small desk in the corner contained a newer model MacBook and a few magazines which, when she leafed through them, she found was a mixture of pornography and weapons-related titles—*Guns and Ammo, Tactical Weapons,* and so on.

She opened the laptop and powered it up, unsurprised to find that it was password protected. There was a notepad by the laptop, the top page blank, but clearly missing some pages. She picked it up and looked to the first empty page. There were clear indentations in the paper, indicating that something had been written on the page above it before it had been torn off. It was hard to make out all of it, but she was pretty sure it read: *Mon. 5:45. CI—Bronx. Rm 202*

It read almost like a puzzle as far as Kate was concerned. It actually made her pretty sure she had read it wrong. But she checked it one more time and found that she had read it right.

She studied it a while longer. Today was Monday. If the *Mon* on that note meant today, then Zeus had left this very apartment at some point today with an appointment somewhere in the Bronx at 5:45. Somewhere with a Room 202. It sounded like a motel room somewhere.

A stirring of excitement started to take over, making her feel certain that whatever had been written was important—that she might be holding something incredibly helpful. *CI, CI, what the hell is CI?*

CI. Room 202. 5:45. Where would a man like Zeus—a man who was presumably a hitman or something similar—be meeting that had the letters CI? Or the initials.

Okay, maybe an apartment complex with the initials CI...

No, the note says room *202, not* apartment *202.*

The answer came barreling at her like a train. She tossed the pad back on the desk and bolted out of the bedroom, directly toward the front door. On the way down the stairs back out to the street, she pulled up Google and typed in two words under a search within the Bronx: *Comfort Inn.*

***

She sped along the way, fully prepared to show her badge and ID if she was pulled over by local law enforcement. She'd been enough similar situations in the past to know that most cops wouldn't think twice about it when they saw a woman flashing FBI credentials. She was speeding not only in the hopes of getting to the Comfort Inn before whatever meeting Zeus was having was over, but because the day was wearing her out. Her drives, first out to the firing range and then to Buckingham Correction Center, felt like they had occurred three or four days ago, a sign that this very long day was catching up to her.

She pulled her car into the lot of the Comfort Inn seventeen minutes later, once again feeling quite fortunate that she did not live in New York and have to put up with the miserable traffic and busyness. Her nerves were starting to fire on all cylinders as she strode up the exterior stairs and to the open-air corridor that contained the majority of the second floor.

She took a deep breath, steadying herself as she came to Room 202. The fact that she had followed him here, based on his own personal notes, would be all the evidence Zeus would need to know that he was being investigated. There was a very good chance that this confrontation would get heated—maybe even violent.

Shit, she thought, hesitating at the door.

She then strolled by the window of the room, hoping to be able to peer inside. But the curtains were drawn and she could see nothing. With no other course of action to take, she steeled her nerves and knocked.

Just like the apartment, there was no answer. She knocked again, this time giving up on any sort of subtlety. "Mr. Beringer, it's very important that you open the door."

When there was still no answer, she looked back down to the parking lot and the neon Office sign. She went back down the stairs and into the office. A man dressed in a hooded sweatshirt sat behind the desk, typing something into an old laptop. Beside him, a woman was speaking to someone on a landline phone.

"Can I help you?" the man in the hoodie asked.

Kate showed her ID right away, not wanting to beat around the bush with formalities. "I'm Special Agent Kate Wise with the FBI," she said. "I need to know who is currently in Room 202."

The woman on the phone had taken an interest in the conversation. She was apparently the manager because she gave the man in the hoodie a shake of the head after looking closely at Kate's ID.

"That's private information, ma'am. I can't just give that out." He looked back to the manager, still on the phone. "Doesn't she need a warrant?"

The manager quickly ended her call and came to his aid. "Yes, you need a warrant," she said.

"Fine," Katye replied. "I'll get a warrant. And by that time, there will be enough police officers in the know. I'll have probably a dozen or so around here, in the parking lot—for everyone to see. Or, you can let me up there right now, just me, to keep it nice and quiet."

The manager sighed, looked to Kate's ID again, and nodded. "Go ahead."

The man typed something into the laptop, studied the screen for a moment, and said: "Adam Smith."

A fake name if I've ever heard one, she thought. "How did he pay?"

"Cash."

"Can you tell me when he checked in?"

Again, he studied the screen. "Five thirty-six."

"I've tried knocking on the door and there is no answer," Kate said. "I need a key to that room."

The woman strode over to the computer and looked over the information while the man in the hoodie retrieved a room key for Kate. "He called about the room yesterday afternoon. Reserved it for tonight."

The man handed Kate the key and she headed straight back out to the parking lot with a quick "Thank you," over her shoulder.

She wasn't quite as hesitant as she reached Room 202 this time. She went directly to the door. Before unlocking it though, she stood there for a moment, listening for any sounds from inside. After ten seconds of silence had passed, she inserted the key, turned it, and stepped inside.

She took one step in and froze.

She wasn't sure what she had been expecting, but it certainly had not been this.

With a trembling hand, she shut the door behind her. She then turned on the light and tried to make sense of what had happened to the dead body on the floor.

CHAPTER FOURTEEN

The man had been shot four times. One shot had gone perfectly through his throat and another had entered his face just below the right eye. The other two were almost directly beside one another, high up on his chest. Kate saw that the one under his eye had gone in at an angle—probably the one that had killed him before he'd had time to choke from the one through the neck.

She had plenty of time to access the scene; between the time she'd called the NYPD and the arrival of the first patrol car, she'd had a whole five minutes alone with the body. While she'd waited for the police to arrive, one of the things she'd done was check the man's wallet, which she found in his back right pocket.

The dead man on the floor was Malcom Z. Beringer.

The scene seemed pretty cut-and-dried at first—a dead body told the story pretty perfectly—but Kate quickly put a few other pieces together. First, the gunshot wounds looked identical to the one in the back of Jack Tucker's head. The only real difference was the amount of gore present at this scene; the shot that had torn through his neck had produced quite a bit of blood—blood that was still wet.

Apparently, someone had called and asked to meet him here. And he had been killed for his troubles. Killed by someone who apparently did not participate in whatever weird code most hitmen had. The four shots, all scattered around the body, indicated that whoever did this had not been a pro.

When she looked around the room, she saw the butt of a gun sticking out from under the bed. She pulled it out with the tip of her shoe, not wanting to contaminate it with her fingerprints. She was not a gun expert, but she was pretty sure the gun currently sitting on the floor was the one she had mentioned so often over the course of the last few days: A Ruger Hunter Mark IV. It was equipped with a silencer.

The police had arrived as she had been checking out the bathroom. There was a single damp washcloth hanging on the side of the tub but other than that, the place seemed unused.

"Agent Wise?" an officer called.

She joined the officer and two others that came in behind him. They were crowding the doorway as the third officer closed it.

"You know him?" the officer asked.

"Not personally. No. But he was a point of interest in a case concerning the murder of Jack Tucker right here in New York a few days ago. His name is Malcom Beringer—known to some unscrupulous characters as Zeus."

"You think he killed Tucker?" the officer asked.

"I don't know. But what I do know is that this Comfort Inn and this room number were written on a pad at his house. He was to meet someone here at five forty-five this afternoon. Whoever reserved the room checked in under the alias of Adam Smith."

"There was a local detective that was handling that Tucker case. Luke Pritchard. You want me to get him in on this?"

She thought it would be a smart idea but she was also very aware that she had discovered this body while not assigned to any particular case. Rather than dig her potential grave any deeper, she decided to play it safe.

"Run it however you'd like," she said. "I need to step out and call my director."

The officer nodded and the others parted to let her out of the room. She walked back out into the open-air corridor. She wasn't sure if it was her nerves or the approaching fall starting to make itself known in the air along the upper East Coast, but Kate felt a little chill. She knew what she had to do and although she hated to admit it to herself, she was a little afraid.

She pulled out her cell phone and dialed up Duran. She didn't bother with his office number, opting to go straight for his mobile.

"This is Duran," he said. The tone in his voice indicated that he was a little irritated. Perhaps he'd seen her name and number on the display before answering.

"It's Kate," she said. "I know I'm no longer on the case, but I feel I should let you know that I'm currently standing outside of a motel where a man has just been killed. A man that very likely owned and was killed by the same sort of gun that killed Jack Tucker and Frank Nobilini."

The three seconds of silence that followed this was heavy. When Duran finally spoke, there was a growl to his voice, the tone of a beast that had been nudged by a curious kid with a stick.

"Where are you?"

"New York. The Bronx."

"And what the hell are you doing there?" The rage in his voice was like a quiet lion, slinking through the grass on the hunt.

She did her best to walk him through the course of her day. From her revelation about speaking with Alvin Carpenter, to finding the information about Zeus's meeting at this Comfort Inn, from discovering the body and the gun to calling in the local cops. The only thing she left out was the bit of assistance she had gotten from DeMarco.

"That's all fascinating and promising," Duran said. "But you seem to be omitting the fact that you are there against my orders. You were here—present and accounted for and of a sound mind when I removed you from the case, correct?"

"Yes sir. And I apologize. But I think this murder and the gun involved…I think it points to something big in this case."

"You understand that had you done this while on active duty, you'd be suspended, right?"

"I do. And you can do whatever you feel you need to. I understand. But I'm here. Right now, I'm here in the middle of it. I just ask that you let me keep digging. Sir…the blood in that room is still fresh. He hasn't been dead for long. Whoever did it can't have gotten far."

"And what will you do when you find them? Have you considered that this man may have nothing to do with the Jack Tucker case?"

"I have. But the gun, sir. It's the exact same kind Jack Tucker and Frank Nobilini were killed with. The chances of that happening and me finding it…it feels related."

Duran let out a shaky sigh. She could nearly hear him gripping the phone tightly in frustration.

"What's the guy's full name?"

"Malcolm Zeus Beringer."

"Got an address?"

"Plugged into my GPS. I'll text it to you."

"Do that. I'll get someone on this…checking his cell phone records, criminal profile, the works. Give us until midnight. Kate…you do what you think needs to be done but you are walking on eggshells, you understand? And when this is over, you and I are going to have to have a serious fucking talk. Am I understood?"

"Yes sir."

"Good." And with that, he ended the call.

Kate relaxed a bit. While the conversation had gone much better than she had expected, her nerves were still chaotic. If nothing else, though, she now had a huge motivator going into the final stages of this case: based on Duran's reaction, it might very well be the last one she ever worked on.

CHAPTER FIFTEEN

The next several hours passed by in a flurry of activity. The police decided it would be more efficient to call in Detective Luke Pritchard and have him run the show, giving assistance where it was needed. A small base of sorts was set up in the parking lot of the Comfort Inn, where Pritchard tasked some of the officers were small jobs. He was taking charge within seconds of arriving on the scene. Kate was coming out of the main office as he started working things out, impressed with how well he worked with the cops.

She walked over, fully prepared to show her badge and ID. But before she could, Pritchard looked her way and gave a smile of acknowledgment. "Agent Wise," he said. "I hear you were the one that found the body?"

"That's correct."

"How did you manage that? The PD have told me a few details but that's about it."

She found herself again running through a quick breakdown of how she had come to Room 202 of the Bronx Comfort Inn. Pritchard took a few handwritten notes in a small ledger as she did so. When she was done, he scanned his notes, nodding here and there.

"I'll stop by his apartment and see what we can pull from that laptop. Any word on the gun you found?" "Almost certain it was the same kind used to murder Jack Tucker. It's been bagged and is on the way to the station."

"Great. And what are you up to right now?"

"I just finished speaking with the manager. They're rolling back through security camera footage from this afternoon to see if there's anything that might help to explain what happened. I've already got the bureau working on pulling up phone records and getting a criminal profile."

"Great. The blood in there...it's too fresh. I think if we work together on this, we can wrap it by morning."

"Let's hope so," Kate said.

"Agent?"

They both turned to the sound of the voice from behind them. It was the motel manager, standing by the front door of the office. She was waving Kate forward, a look of reserved anxiety on her face.

Kate assumed it was not in the motel's best interests to have a murder investigation going on as it got later and later into the night.

"Let me check the footage," Kate said. "If there's anything worth noting, I'll let you know."

"Let me get your number then. I'll do the same if we can manage to get anything off of Beringer's laptop."

They exchanged numbers before Kate left him to his business. She headed inside the main office where the manager was waiting for her. She led Kate around the back of the check-in counter to where a small office was set up. The manager allowed Kate to sit in the chair behind the desk while she navigated around the security camera software. She showed Kate the ropes quickly—how to fast forward, freeze frame, zoom in, rewind, and so on.

Kate had used countless different security interfaces before so learning this one was rather simple. The set-up was only one screen, one view, but it was from the right edge of the property, taking in nearly the entire parking lot. The manager had brought her back to 5:30—six minutes before the so-called Adam Smith had checked into Room 202. Kate fast-forwarded through the next few minutes, stopping whenever she saw a car park in the lot. There were two that parked in front of the motel between 5:30 and 5:36. One was a man dressed in a button-down shirt and a pair of slacks. Another looked to be a mother and her young daughter, aged ten or so. Other than those two occurrences, there was nothing. She went back to the 5:30 mark and watched the entire thing again, this time at regular speed. She thought maybe someone had simply walked up. But after watching the footage, all she saw was a stray shadow that seemed to pass beneath the camera's angle. It could have been a person, she just wasn't sure.

Kate walked back out of the office, joining the manager back behind the desk. On the other side of the lobby, a policeman was interviewing the clerk in the hoodie—the man Kate had spoken to when she'd come in to get the key.

"Excuse me," Kate said as she walked toward the manager. "On the footage, I see a mother and daughter pair and then a single man that park, get out of their cars, and come into the office. I never see the man that I found upstairs. Can you check your logs and see how many people did indeed check in in those six minutes?"

"I've got it up right here," she said, pointing to her laptop. "I figured that would be the next thing you ask. There were three rooms that were checked into during that time. Two of those rooms were the mother and daughter and the single man. The third was Adam Smith."

82

"Did *you* check him in?"

"I did."

"Can you describe him for me?"

The manager took a moment to think back, shrugging. "Nothing special about him, really. Mid-fifties, I guess. Slight scruff on his face but not really a beard. Plain hair. Nothing special."

Kate nodded. She was describing Malcolm Z. Beringer to a tee. "Do you know if he was carrying anything?"

"I didn't take notice, honestly. I don't recall anything."

Kate stood there a moment, thinking. A man like Beringer would know to be aware of security cameras wherever he went. She wondered if he had parked somewhere nearby and walked to the motel, perhaps coming up along the side and walking very closely along the exterior walls. If he'd come in from the left side of the building, this would have just barely put him out of range of the security camera.

But the question still remained, even if he managed to get into the motel undetected by the cameras: who had he met with and how did they get in unseen as well? Did they go in *with* Beringer? If both parties were being careful, that was the most likely scenario.

She thanked the manager for her assistance and then headed back outside. The little makeshift base had mostly broken up. A few officers remained by a single car while another was upstairs along the breezeway, standing guard by the door. Kate assumed that Detective Pritchard had already left to take the laptop from Beringer's apartment. She made her way upstairs, the man by the door nodding to her and stepping aside.

"We're okay to the call the coroner now," she told him. "I think the body has told us just about everything it's going to tell us."

"Sure," the officer said and headed down to join the others.

Kate opened the door to Room 202 and stepped inside again. She retraced her steps from before, observing the room as slowly and as methodically as possible. The manager said she had not seen whether or not Beringer had been carrying a suitcase or bag and as far as Kate could tell, he had not. There was no luggage of any kind in the room.

She stood by the door, taking the size and dimensions of the room in. She looked to the TV and the small dresser it sat on. She looked to the bed and...

She paused there. She had noticed the sheets had been slightly unmade the first time she had looked the room over but now they seemed a little more relevant. The untidy nature of the sheets indicated that someone had done more than simply sit there. The bottom sheet was pulled tight and the top sheet—what passed for a comforter at the Comfort Inn, apparently—had been pushed hard to the left. It might seem flimsy to most but as far as she was concerned, that was evidence of a struggle. And that meant that Zeus Beringer had not simply walked blindly into the room and had someone unload on him. There had indeed been some sort of meeting before he was killed. Kate kept going back to the four shots, scattered almost randomly, and was certain the killer had been someone who was not a pro.

If we find out who killed him, that's going to lead to all the right answers, she thought. And even though there were no hard solid links, her gut told her that at the bottom of it all would be the answers she was looking for in the Jack Tucker case.

Now, as Pritchard was looking into the laptop and the gun was being run for prints, there was nothing for her to do but wait.

***

Once the coroner arrived, Kate drove to the local precinct to see what she could do to help expedite the process. As she made her way to the front desk, her phone went off in her pocket. As she answered it, she snuck a glance at the time and was surprised to see that it was already nearing eleven o'clock. She wasn't tired at all now, sensing that there were answers on the horizon.

She was delighted to see that it was DeMarco. "Hey, DeMarco. You didn't get caught assisting me, did you?"

"No. And I'm actually calling to let you know that I'm about to get on yet another plane and head to New York. It seems Duran doesn't quite trust you and wants me to watch after you."

"So you'll be my babysitter?"

"I know you mean that as a joke, but he's really pissed, Kate."

"I gathered that."

"Anyway, I also wanted to let you know that we've still got a team working on the cell phone records. However, we did manage to already get a criminal record on one Malcolm Zeus Beringer. He's a bad dude, that's for sure—or, *was,* I guess. A few B and E's from a young age, two stints in minimum security for basic brawls. Busted about fifteen years ago for carrying an unregistered weapon. He was the suspect in a murder that took place in Albany five years ago but there was never enough evidence to convict."

"Any word on what the unregistered weapon was?"

"A plain everyday nine millimeter. Nothing special. Anything moving there?"

"Detective Pritchard is looking into the laptop I found in Beringer's apartment. I think that and the cell phone records are going to be our best bet." She then took a moment to fill DeMarco in on the state of the body and the room—as well as the discovery of the Ruger just beneath the edge of the bed.

"Yeah, it sounds like a match," DeMarco said. "Just know this: if you've solved this thing by the time I get there, I'll consider this a wasted trip."

"I'll take that into consideration." Her phone dinged at her while it was held to her ear. She took it away from her ear, glanced at it, and saw that it was a text from Duran. **Cellphone records complete,** it read. **Check your e-mail.**

"Gotta go, DeMarco. Duran just texted. Beringer's cell phone records are on the way."

"Good luck with that. See you soon."

They ended the call and Kate walked quickly to the primary front desk in the lobby. Behind the woman at the desk, the precinct was buzzing lightly with pre-midnight activity.

"Can I help you?" the woman at the dispatch desk asked.

"Yes," she said, showing her ID. "I'm Special Agent Wise, working homicide with Detective Pritchard. I have some documents I need to print out from my phone and need access to a printer."

"One moment."

The woman picked up her landline and buzzed someone elsewhere in the precinct. While she waited, Kate did as Duran had instructed. She pulled up her email on her phone and found a new mail with an attachment, straight for Duran's account. She opened the mail, then the PDF attachment, and waited as it loaded.

"Agent Wise?" the woman at the dispatch desk said. "Right this way."

And with that, Kate was led down the hall and toward a small private office. The dispatch worker handed her over to a tech operator in charge of the dispatch network and had her up and running within five minutes, right down to a loaner laptop.

She smiled for just a moment, as a memory of Michael surfaced in her head. He'd always teased her about how when she got really down to the grit and nails of a case, she seemed to have the demeanor and hard-set attitude of all of those New York detectives that were all over primetime TV. And now here she was, working out of an office in a New York City precinct. If there was a heaven, and Kate was of the opinion that there just might be, she hoped he was getting a good glimpse of this.

It was just the bit of motivation she needed as she pulled the cell phone records up on the precinct's borrowed laptop and dove further into whatever secrets Zeus had been hiding.

Secrets she hoped would help her to close not only the Tucker case, but the Nobilini case, thus finally closing a very open scar on her career.

CHAPTER SIXTEEN

It took her less than fifteen minutes to understand that the phone records may prove to be worthless and yet another ten to feel all but *confident* that they had been a waste of time. As she finished looking over them, fully prepared to pull at least a handful of very weak leads from it, there was a knock at the door. She looked up and saw Pritchard standing there.

"You got a sec?" he asked.

"Yeah."

He entered the room and, without another seat to take, simply stood against the wall and showed her the laptop under his arm—the same laptop she had seen when she had been looking through Beringer's apartment.

"All the laptop tells us is that Beringer had a soft spot for Asian pornography. While his history does show recent visits to Craigslist, his email history shows that it was to partake in the NYC singles ads. But here's another thing. He's got the Tor browser downloaded on his computer. He went to some fairly decent lengths to hide it, but it's there."

"Tor...that's dark web stuff, right?"

"Yeah. Tor is the most popular darknet software out there. And naturally, because of the way it works, we're going to have a really hard time figuring out what sort of sites he was visiting." He chuckled and pointed at her. "That's usually where you and your bureau friends come in handy."

"Is having the software enough to safely say that Beringer was a hitman?"

"In a perfect world, sure. But you have to realize that the dark web is very accessible these days. Any curious thirteen-year-old can get on just to look around. There's a whole movement of YouTube people going on just to snoop around and film it. So no...having a darknet browser isn't enough for us to make that assumption. But between the evidence we have, including the exact same gun used to kill Jack Tucker, *plus* the fact that he visited the darknet with some regularity...I'd say it's enough to continue looking into him."

"So is that it?"

"Yes. How about you? Any luck with the cell phone data?"

She shrugged and showed him the printouts. "He only made two calls today. One was to his brother in Florida. And you can see on the records that it's a call he made at least once a week. The other call I had to actually call myself to see who it was. Turns out it's just a garage in the Bronx. They were obviously closed when I called, so I may go by tomorrow just to make sure it's legit."

Pritchard nodded, folding his arms over his chest. "How close did you come to wrapping the Nobilini case when you were originally on it?" he asked.

"Not close at all," she said. "There were no leads, not even a single clue at all outside of knowing the make and model of gun used."

"With this Beringer break, do you feel any closer to solving this one?"

"I just don't know," she said. "I feel like it's moving forward but every single lead I get only takes me to another hopeful moment that, in the end, becomes nothing more than a number to a garage or your darknet software."

"It's tricky," he said. "Knowing that there has to be some answer at the end of it all but having everything presented to you be so basic and boring."

"Yes, it's certainly no—"

She stopped here, struck by that word once again. *Boring.*

Only this time, when the word sped across her brain, she was able to snag it. Before, whenever she'd heard it and thought it meant something, it would get away from here, nothing more than a fuzzy idea with no real edges or substance. But this time she not only snagged it, but she focused on it.

"Agent Wise?"

She ignored Pritchard's voice, slowly sitting up in her chair and putting all of her attention on the memory that came to her. She gave a small smile of frustration as she fully understood the memory and what it would mean.

Another case. Yet *another* case in her past…only this was much farther back than Frank Nobilini or Alvin Carpenter. How long ago had it been, anyway? It felt like another life.

"Twenty years or more," she said out loud, answering her own question.

"Excuse me?" Pritchard said.

"Sorry. Talking to myself. Detective Pritchard, I'm so sorry, but could you give me some privacy? I have an idea I want to run with and if I don't get to it now…"

"Say no more," he said, opening the door. "I know how it feels. I'll be just down the hall if you need me."

With that, he closed the door as he left, leaving Kate alone with her thoughts. She turned toward the laptop and used her cell phone to place a call to the bureau resource desk for the second time in the last few days. She was pretty sure the voice that answered on the other end was the woman that had assisted her the first time.

She gave her badge number and location and then, knowing that she'd be in for a long night, requested assistance to remotely and securely access the bureau's database.

**

The case had occurred twenty-four years ago, when Kate had only been three years deep into her career as an agent with the FBI. She could remember the case well enough, a triple homicide in Georgia, but the names were still muddied by both time and the unreliability of human memory. Therefore, it took her a while to find the case she was looking for. When she opened up the first file, it was like being slapped in the face by her past. The case was old enough to where the only digital files on it were scanned documents and notes, many of which had been written in her own, much younger, hand.

The first victim had been a man named Jimmy Keenan and then, shortly after, his brother and best friend. The investigation had lasted about three days and in the end, the murderer had turned out to be Keenan's wife. When asked why she found it necessary to kill her husband, the answer had been simple enough, albeit a little sad and depressing.

Kate read through it all as she sat at the desk, looking at a scanned picture of the wife's testimony, typed up almost twenty-five years ago.

"Married for sixteen years, and you know what the most exciting moment has been for me over the last five of them? The nights when he goes out and plays poker with his friends. That lets me stay at home and do whatever the hell I want, watch whatever I want. He used to be fun and exciting and he couldn't keep his hands off of me. But lately...he just got very routine. Very boring. Just boring, boring, boring. And when he accused me of not ever wanting to do anything fun...I snapped.

Then, later on further down the testimony, she went on:

"Do you know what it's like to hope day after day that the person you married might resurface? He'd complain sometimes that this wasn't the life he wanted—not the life he'd envisioned for himself. But he never did anything about it. He just sat in it. But I

couldn't do that. Could not live that fucking boring life. God, what a fucking bore he was there at the end. You know what? I take back what I said earlier. The most exciting part of the last five years was slamming those hedge clippers into the side of his head."

She had then gone on to kill his brother, mainly because he was visiting and out in their garage when she had killed her husband. The best friend, she'd said later, was because he'd attempted to rape her during a Christmas party early in her marriage and when she'd told her husband, he hadn't believed her.

Kate read her testimony twice. *Boring. Boring.*

How many people had she spoken to who had described Jack Tucker in that same way?

It might be a stretch, but it felt right...in the same way it had felt right to look into Malcolm Zeus Beringer.

The mere idea of Missy Tucker killing her husband seemed absolutely ridiculous. Sure, she did not know the woman on a personal level, but she had seen all kinds of grief during her career—both genuine and staged. And Missy had been an absolute wreck.

Ah, but maybe there are things about her husband she was blind to in her grief, she thought. *A few days removed, maybe she'll be able to offer something more...*

It was worth a shot. Besides...the Zeus Beringer link was looking to come up at a dead end. What other options did she have?

She sighed, sat back in her chair, and read through the old testimony one more time.

CHAPTER SEVENTEEN

Kate met DeMarco at the airport at 5:45 after catching a few hours of sleep at a hotel near the precinct. She filled DeMarco in on everything she had learned since they last spoke, ending it all with the speculations she'd had after revisiting the files from the case in Georgia twenty-four years ago. She did it while fighting off grogginess. Yes, she could spar in a boxing ring and work as a well-rounded agent, but one thing age was not being kind to her about was in regards to sleep. After fifty-five, she apparently needed at least a solid six hours.

"I see why you might go there," DeMarco said. "But then that means you also need to apply that same filter to the Nobilini murders. We've been working to prove that they're linked but I think this, if anything, might work *against* that."

Kate had considered this but figured it was a bridge they could cross only if some new information was found. "That's true," she conceded. "But if I'm being honest, I'm a little hesitant to ask a grieving widow under what circumstances she *would* have killed her husband."

"Do we know what date the funeral is scheduled for?" DeMarco asked.

"No." She was glad to have DeMarco with her. While she still fully intended to speak with Missy again as soon as possible, DeMarco was grounding her a bit. Perhaps it was because of their little bit of tension following the first visit to the Tucker household wherein they had broken the news of Jack's death and DeMarco's reaction to it. Whatever the reason, Kate could feel more of a balance between them.

As Kate parked in front of the precinct she had spent several hours in the night before, DeMarco was looking over her own notes from the Tucker case. "You know," she said, "I can't help but wonder if there is someone else we can speak to before Missy. I'm not too keen on talking to her right now. Not to take several steps back and get all pissy about it again, but I'd prefer to let her handle the storm of shit that's on her way: the funeral, her kids at the funeral, sleeping alone in that house for the first time after watching her husband's coffin lowered into the ground."

"Jesus, DeMarco, that's grim."

She shrugged. "I know we spoke to Alice Delgado and she gave us the names of Missy's best friends. She mentioned a woman named Jasmine Brooks that we never managed to get in touch with. I say we try her one more time before going straight to Missy."

Kate nodded her agreement as they got out of the car and headed inside. She felt rushed and even a little off her game in that DeMarco had recalled the name Jasmine Brooks while she, Kate, had let it fall by the wayside. Sure, she'd had a lot to deal with since then—being pulled off of the case, visiting Alvin Carpenter, and then discovering Zeus Beringer's body—but she should not have simply overlooked a potential lead, no matter now sure she was that it would pan out to nothing.

Kate led DeMarco back to her little private office. DeMarco took a quick look around at some of the work Kate had done the night before. The printouts from the old Georgia case, a borrowed whiteboard with checklists and a link-chart, most of which has been marked through, and the little desk, complete with the laptop and an empty coffee cup.

"I see you made yourself at home here," DeMarco said.

"I'd hate to see what your home looks like," Kate quipped.

"So all we're waiting on are forensics reports from the gun, right?"

"For right now, yes."

"And you've been working closely with Pritchard?"

"Not closely. He ran the laptop check while we were waiting on the phone records."

"I see," DeMarco said.

Her hint of teasing was clear in her voice, making it known that she rather liked the idea of Kate working with Pritchard. Kate nearly commented on it, but let it go. It would only lead to a good-natured conversation about her love life and right now, given the nature of the last conversation she'd had with Allen, that was not something she wanted to get into.

"So, Jasmine Brooks," Kate said, before DeMarco had the opportunity to venture any further into that territory. "Let's get an address and pay her a visit. But if nothing comes of that, I think we *have* to speak with Missy."

"I can live with that," DeMarco said. "You start digging for the address. As for me, with that red-eye flight and very little sleep under my belt, I'll take charge of coffee duty."

***

Jasmine Brooks lived in a two-story house on a secluded plot of open land in one of the nicer parts of Ashton. When Kate and DeMarco pulled their car into the Brooks' driveway, Jasmine was standing on the porch, watching her child—a girl of about twelve or so—as she stood at the end of the driveway. Given that Kate had gotten behind two different school buses on her way out to Ashton, she assumed the child was waiting for the bus.

Jasmine Brooks gave them a peculiar look as they got out of the car and started walking toward the porch. She almost looked afraid, Kate thought. She was inching toward forty with a headful of gorgeous blonde hair and a figure that most healthy twenty-one-year-old women would covet.

"Can I help you ladies?" Jasmine asked before they even reached the porch.

Kate revealed her ID as subtly as she could, not wanting the child at the end of the driveway to see. "Agents Wise and DeMarco, with the FBI." She looked back out to the kid along the end of the driveway and asked: "Waiting for the bus?"

"Yeah. She does that and I drink my cup of coffee on the porch. It's our little morning ritual. Until the weather gets cold, anyway."

As she said this, a county school bus came around the bend, slowing to a stop. Kate extended the courtesy of allowing Jasmine to watch her daughter get on the bus before getting into her questions. Her daughter turned and waved before getting on the bus. As it started accelerating down the road to the next stop, Kate nodded up the porch stairs.

"Can we come up? We'd like to ask you some questions about Jack and Missy Tucker."

Jasmine's frown was immediate, but she nodded. "They still don't know who did it?"

"Not yet, no," Kate asked. "And we're trying to learn more about Missy and Jack as we get further along. We keep hearing the same things—how they were a perfect couple, how they were great together, how Jack was this impossibly kind man. So kind and straight down the middle that some have gone go far as to refer to him as *boring*."

Jasmine chuckled, but stopped it before it could sound anything close to happy. "That's a little unfair, though I suppose I can understand that."

"We understand you are very close with Missy," DeMarco said.

"Yeah," Jasmine said, though there wasn't much enthusiasm in her voice. "We've known each other since high school. Some would say we were best friends."

"Were?" Kate asked.

Jasmine sighed and sat down in a white wicker rocker. She rocked slightly as she held her cup of coffee. "Yeah. Missy and I haven't really been very friendly as of late."

"Any reason?"

Jasmine was quiet for a while. It was clear that she was struggling not to weep. In the end, about ten seconds after the battle started, she lost. A few stray tears went rolling down her cheeks. She didn't bother wiping them away.

"I don't want to spread her business," she finally said.

"We can respect that," Kate said. "But at the risk of sounding cold, hearing that they were perfect and that Jack was an incredible man isn't helping us. He was killed for a reason. And any secrets they might have been keeping—or secrets about them individually that their family and friends might know—are huge stepping stones towards finding out what happened...and why."

Jasmine gripped the edges of the armrests on the rocker and whispered a curse.

"It's okay," DeMarco said. "You can remain anonymous."

Jasmine shook her head. "No I can't. I'm the only one that knows."

Kate and DeMarco remained quiet, giving Jasmine the time and space she needed. Kate could tell by the look of guilt on Jasmine's face that she was going to tell them what she knew; it was just a case of getting beyond the guilt to share it.

"It was about six months ago," Jasmine finally said. "Maybe a little less. We would usually meet for lunch when she was free on Wednesdays. We'd always meet at the same place—Emmanuel Bakery and Kitchenette—at the same time. Twelve thirty, Wednesday afternoon. But she called me one Wednesday morning and asked if we could meet here, at my house, instead. I told her sure, and that's what we did. We had lunch right at my kitchen table. She told me she had to tell me something—something that was going to kill her to get out. I gave her some time and she started crying before it came. She told me that she had done something awful, something she couldn't forgive herself for."

Jasmine stopped here, struggling with more tears. Kate already knew where it was going; she'd heard it countless times in her career. But she needed to hear it from Jasmine Brooks for it to mean anything.

94

"She said she'd been having an affair. Not just a one-time thing, either. She never gave me a number, but she said it was several times. She was wrecked about it."

"Was she actively involved in it when she told you?" Kate asked.

"She said she'd ended it the week before and that he was in agreement."

"Do you know why they ended the affair?" DeMarco asked.

"I think that's what hurt her the most...why it was so hard on her," Jasmine said. "She said it was purely physical at first. The kind of sex women assume is long gone after thirty. But she said over time, there was an emotional connection. Not just on her part. It was mutual. They were falling in love."

"Who was the affair with?" Kate asked.

Again, it was clear that Jasmine did not want to reveal this information. She had finally started to wipe away some of the tears that were falling, giving in to the fact that she was losing the mental wrestling match within her heart.

"Garret Blake." She said the name as if it were a curse word, slowly and softly, looking away from them as if ashamed.

"And are you sure you're the only person she told?"

"At the time she told me, I know I was. She made it a very clear point to let me know that. But in the time that passed between then and now, I can't say for certain."

"So we've gathered that you *used* to be friends with Missy Tucker," DeMarco said. "What happened to the friendship?"

Jasmine shrugged. "She became distant after she told me. And it got worse week after week. I think the guilt or shame or whatever kept her away. I tried reaching out, but she ignored me. When we'd pass by each other at school functions for the kids, she'd basically just ignore me."

"Do you know Garret Blake?"

"Not well. I see him at school functions from time to time as well."

"So he lives in Ashton?"

"He does. But he works in the city. Co-owner of a trendy little marketing firm. Look...I know you have to do your job and all, but if you could somehow *not* let it be known that I gave you this information..."

"We'll be very discreet if it does come up," Kate said. "Ms. Brooks, thank you for your time. And thank you for sharing. I know it wasn't easy."

She nodded and then, as the agents were headed down their stairs, called out with one last detail to share. "I can sort of see where you're trying to go with this," she said. "But from what I know of Missy Tucker and Garret Blake, I can pretty much guarantee you that neither of them would be capable of killing."

"We'll keep that under consideration," Kate said.

But even she could hear the doubt in her tone. Because if nearly three decades in the bureau had taught her anything, it was that just about anyone was capable of *anything* if they were trying to hide a damning secret.

CHAPTER EIGHTEEN

The marketing firm that Garret Blake worked for was called One-Up. It was located in Manhattan, in one of the trendier little nooks where everything seemed to be bookended by coffee shops, music stores that were stocked full with vinyl, and expensive juice bars. They found the place easy enough and by 9:45, Kate was parking in a small garage across the street from the building One-Up was located in.

The interior was cute and welcoming, decorated mostly with glass walls and bright blasts of color with encouraging phrases. The woman at the welcome desk was in her mid-twenties with a nose ring, an eyebrow ring, and a shock of bright purple in her black hair.

"Can I help you?" the secretary asked.

"We need to speak with Garret Blake," DeMarco said.

"Do you have an appointment?"

"No," Kate said. "But he's going to want to talk with us."

"Can I ask what this is in regards to?"

"No."

The girl looked at them awkwardly, apparently never having caught any sort of attitude from women older than her before.

"One moment, please," she said. She got up, walking behind one of the glass doors and into an office on the far side of the workspace.

"You ever have hair like that when you were younger?" Kate asked DeMarco.

"I did, actually. Red tips. But that was also around the time I was wearing blood red lipstick and wearing chokers with little spikes on them, so…"

"I'd like a picture of that someday, please."

"I don't think so."

The camaraderie was brought to an end when they saw the secretary coming out of the office with a man trailing behind her. He was a younger man, maybe thirty-five or so. He was the sort of guy who managed to look ruggedly handsome thanks to the scruff on his face and the broadness of his neck and shoulders, yet also looked modern and sophisticated because of his sleek yet semi-casual attire.

97

He greeted them with a smile as he came to the front desk. He looked them over for a moment, trying to place their faces. "What can I do for you ladies?" Garret asked.

"We were hoping to speak with you," DeMarco said. "For just a moment."

"And preferably in private," Kate said. She pushed some edginess into her tone, hoping he'd feel the urgency in it. She really didn't want to have to show her ID in front of the secretary; she wanted to be able to keep this as quiet as possible. But if she had to pull her ID, she most certainly would.

"Yes, that's fine. We can meet in my office. But I do have a conference call I need to be a part of in fifteen minutes."

"I don't think it will quite that long," Kate said.

He turned away quickly, something Kate could not help but take notice of. He led them around the first glass partition and through the tidy industrial-looking workspace. His office was just as tidy—perfectly smooth edges and a complete lack of clutter anywhere. He closed the door behind him and walked to his desk while they took two of the three guest chairs in front of his desk.

"You detectives?" he asked without waiting a single moment.

"No," Kate said, finally pulling her ID. "FBI. I'm Agent Wise and this is Agent DeMarco. What made you instantly assume we were detectives?"

"The way you're dressed," he said. But he then leaned back nervously in his chair and started to look antsy. "And if I'm being honest, I've been expecting the police or a detective or someone to show these last few days."

"Why is that?" Kate asked. She wanted him to offer as much information as possible without having to guide or bully him into doing so.

"Well, I know that Jack Tucker was murdered. I didn't know him well but if you are here in regards to that, I'm assuming that you somehow found out that I know his wife quite well."

"That's all correct," Kate said. "And it took us a while to find that out. In fact, we were told that Jack and Missy Tucker had a perfect marriage."

"They did, from the outside. Great house, great kids, great people. What I knew of Jack, he really was a stand-up guy. But I think under the surface, the marriage had gone sort of stale. Missy never gave me any details. She just said there was no excitement. No passion or fun. She said things had gotten predictable and boring."

"How did the affair start?" Kate asked.

Garret sighed and looked away. So far, he had not spoken with any sign of true regret, nor did he particularly seem proud of what he had done. But now he seemed to be wrestling with something. Perhaps whether or not to share the details of his affair with Missy Tucker.

"Look...I've made mistakes. I look back on them now and am ashamed. I was married when the affair happened. Still am...to the same woman. She doesn't have to find out about this, does she?"

"Not unless you turn out to be a likely suspect," Kate said.

Relief flashed across his face instantly. It was nearly enough to make Kate feel as if he wasn't a suspect at all. He was just lucky to have dodged another bullet that could have ended his marriage.

Poor woman, Kate thought, thinking of his wife.

"She came here, looking for pricing on brochures for the middle school band," Blake said. "An errand for the PTA. Usually a woman named Melissa Carter handles it, but she was on the verge of having a baby and I think Missy was sort of just filling in. She hated it. She was very uncomfortable with the responsibility of it all. Now, she and I have never truly known one another—just in passing at school and there were two times where Jack and I both helped work on the elementary school Christmas float for the Ashton Christmas parade. When we were wrapping up the meeting, I offhandedly asked how Jack was. And I don't know...it sort of devolved into this spiel about how he seemed like a different person. I myself was divorced ten years ago, so I knew what she was talking about. My first wife sort of just drifted off. We ended things amicably after just two years. No hard feelings. We knew we were growing apart and that was that. So I gave her some advice...advice, I might add, that was intended to help her heal whatever was wrong with her marriage.

"Anyway, she came back in the following week to place the order and to go over color schemes and all of that. She thanked me for talking to her the week before and asked that I please not tell anyone about it. I assured her I wouldn't. And...hell, I don't know. Honestly can't even recall how it happened. One minute I'm standing right there beside her, showing her a sample of another brochure on my computer and the next, I'm turning around and we're sort of pressing into each other. It was heated and quick...right here, in the office."

"How long ago was this?" Kate asked.

"Maybe a little over a year ago."

"We understand it wasn't a one-time thing," DeMarco said. "What happened after that first encounter?"

"It was two weeks later. Someone knocked on my door at home, at six or seven in the afternoon. It was Missy. She'd only come because she knew my wife was out of town on business. She said she'd been thinking about what we had done, but not in a shameful way. She said it made her excited when she thought about it. I agreed. And that was the second time it happened. When it was over, we decided to try to make a run of it...an affair, in secret of course."

This infuriated Kate but she had to remind herself that not everyone held the same set of morals she did. So she tried to keep things as civil as possible by asking: "Did you have no qualms about sleeping with a married woman?"

"Oh no, I did. We nearly ended it several times. Guilt finally caught up with both of us. It almost ended several times but...I think after several months we both started to understand that it was becoming something more than just a physical relationship. And *that's* when she truly got scared."

"Did she ever talk about leaving Jack for you?" Kate asked.

"A few times." He paused here, clearly uncomfortable, and then added: "You have to understand, I don't enjoy sharing this...especially in light of what happened. But I was ready to leave my wife for her. To answer your question...yes, I think if she didn't have kids with him, she would have left him."

"And would you have taken her?" Kate asked.

'I believe I would have. I have no problem admitting to myself that I was starting to fall in love with her."

"Was there any conflict when it came to an end?"

"No. She said she knew if we kept doing it, she'd let her feelings override her logic and she'd get caught. And she did not want to put her kids through that."

"And you just let it end?" DeMarco asked. "Just like that?"

"Yes. Look...I'm not proud of the affair. And while I still have strong feelings for her and I enjoyed our time together...I'm not a big enough asshole to be the man that causes a family to deteriorate."

Kate believed him but was still not confident in the fact that he was innocent. If he did indeed still have feelings for Missy, that alone would give him motivation to kill her husband.

"Mr. Blake, do you own any guns?" she asked.

"No. I used to. Actually, it was my first wife's. She hated to have it, but she claimed it made her feel safe. She took it with her when she left."

"Have you ever fired one?" DeMarco asked.

"Sure. My father was into hunting. We spent one week each summer for about three years or so in a cabin in Maine, hunting deer. But that was when I was like thirteen or so. I don't think I've even touched a gun since then." He seemed to understand where the line of questioning was leading; a look of sour disgust came over his face. "Are you seriously considering the fact that I killed Jack?"

"Given your recent history with his wife, you understand how we would have to at least consider the option," Kate said.

He nodded, though the look on his face indicated that he felt offended. "So long as you can keep the news of the affair away from his family and those closest to them, you're welcome to look into whatever you need. My home, my phone, whatever. I'll cooperate within reason."

"We appreciate that," Kate said. Before getting up, one last thing came to her. She was thinking of small towns like Ashton and the process of gossip being spread. "I can't tell you how we found out about the affair," she said. "But is there anyone you know of that would have known about it?"

"Well, I think Patricia, the secretary you encountered out front, was suspicious. But she never actually *knew*. And I certainly never told anyone. I can't say for certain who Missy told."

With that, Kate finally allowed herself to stand. DeMarco, apparently having no further questions either, did the same.

"We appreciate your time and honesty," Kate said. She then handed him her business card and added: "But if you *are* keeping anything from us that you just can't bring yourself to admit, please call me if you decided to come clean. Any potential sources of new information for this case would be extremely helpful."

"I give you my word that I've told you everything."

Kate only nodded as she took her leave. As she and DeMarco walked through the workspace and to the doors beyond, the secretary eyed them suspiciously. She gave them a hesitant wave goodbye as they headed through the doors.

Back out on the street, DeMarco's entire mood seemed to change instantly. Her shoulders slumped and she was looking down to the ground.

"DeMarco? You okay?" Kate asked.

"No. I think he was telling the truth. So if we want to know if there was anyone else that might have known about the affair, I know who we have to ask next. And it sucks."

"I know," Kate said, and left it that.

They got into the car and headed out of the city in silence. And the closer they got back toward Ashton, the heavier that silence became.

CHAPTER NINETEEN

As they drew closer to the Tucker residence, Kate noticed that DeMarco seemed to be growing more and more anxious. As they turned onto the street Missy Tucker lived on, DeMarco pulled out her cell phone. Kate listened with a heavy heart as DeMarco spoke to the director of Ashton's only funeral home.

It hurt Kate to hear the conversation—almost as much as the fact that she knew that DeMarco would soon grow out of this uneasiness. Soon, she'd learn to roll with these sorts of punches…to be able to put common decency and kindness on the back burner for the sake of the case. It was something most agents simply grew desensitized to. For Kate, it had happened after the first three or four years, case after case that required her to question grieving family members with some very hard questions. She admired the spark of decency in DeMarco and wondered how much longer she'd be able to hang on to it.

"Tomorrow," DeMarco said. "Jack's body was released to the funeral home today and the service is scheduled for tomorrow afternoon. And we're about to go throw an affair in his wife's face."

"I'm not looking forward to it either," Kate said.

"I know. It just…God, it sucks."

That was the last thing said on the topic. Kate pulled her car up alongside the curb in front of the Tucker house. They got out of the car and walked up to the house slowly. Kate knocked on the door, DeMarco keeping a step or two of distance between them.

The door was answered by the daughter. Kate could not recall the girl's name but knew that she was thirteen and a dead ringer for her mother. Without so much as waiting for Kate or DeMarco to say anything, the girl turned and called for her mother, walking back into the house.

Within a few seconds, Missy Tucker was walking toward the door. She looked much better that she had three nights ago. She looked better rested but still quite forlorn. She looked surprised to see the agents, though Kate could not tell if it was a hopeful sort of surprise or an aggravated one.

"Agents…" she said, clearly at a loss.

"Mrs. Tucker, I do apologize for bothering you again," Kate said. "But we were hoping we could speak to you for just a few moments."

"Did you find…someone? Did you find out who killed him?"

"I'm afraid not," Kate said. "But we have come across new information we were hoping to discuss with you."

Missy nodded and invited them in. Inside, the house still felt cold and lonely. Kate had always thought there was an almost supernatural sort of sensation in a house that had just suffered the loss of a major inhabitant—something dreary and detached that crawled on the skin like dew.

Missy led them into the living room and headed straight for the couch. Kate and DeMarco sat down—DeMarco on the couch with Missy, and Kate in an armchair to the right of it.

"Mrs. Tucker," Kate said, "did you ever hear about the Frank Nobilini case from several years back?"

"You know…I did, but I didn't even make the connection," she said. "I recall you telling me that Jack's murder was very similar to another one that had occurred, but I was in such a state of shock that I didn't even stop to consider that you were referencing Frank Nobilini's murder."

"Do you know Jennifer Nobilini very well?" DeMarco asked.

"Pretty well. We're about ten years apart in age, so we never knew one another in school. But some of our social circles interact from time to time. We've never really had much in common but we're decent friends, I suppose. Well, now I suppose the thing we have in common is what happened to our husbands. She called to check in with me after she'd heard what happened. She can sympathize, obviously."

"That was kind of her," Kate said.

"It was. Now…what new information have you come across?"

Kate took a moment before she started. She listened out for the children. She could hear footsteps upstairs somewhere, and a light murmur of conversation somewhere in the downstairs. She leaned forward and tried to keep her voice as quiet as she could without being reduced to a whisper.

"We just came from the city," she said. "From a meeting with Garret Blake."

Even if Missy would have played dumb on the topic, the immediate reaction to the mention of that name gave her away. She reeled back, her lips began to tremble, and her eyes grew wide for a moment before returning to their normal size. To say the name had shocked her would have been an understatement.

"Why?" was all she managed to say, the word coming out in a gasp. She continued to tremble, now clenching her fists in an attempt to steady herself.

"It's where our trail led us," Kate said. "And please understand that we aren't bringing this up to cause you any more pain but we *do* need to know a few things about what occurred between the two of you."

"What good would that do?" Missy asked. She was crying now and the expression on her face made Kate think that she was doing her absolute best to decide if she wanted to be pissed off or devastated.

"It would help us rule out certain people as suspects and—"

"He didn't do anything to Jack. He wanted to me to stay with him—to keep my kids happy and my family together." She was nearly spitting the words now, becoming more and more aggressive.

"Mrs. Tucker," DeMarco said, her tone just as soft as Kate's. "Can you at the very least tell us who might have known about the affair?"

"Well, I think you know at least one," Missy said with biting sarcasm and bitterness. "It was Jasmine, wasn't it? I'm sure she couldn't wait to tell someone."

"She was actually very upset to tell us," Kate countered. "And the only reason she did is because she is concerned about you."

"Garret Blake did not kill my husband," she said. "I highly doubt the man has ever touched a gun." She seemed to realize that she was speaking rather loudly, so she quieted her voice and leaded forward on the couch. She took a deep breath and the anger seemed to fade as she exhaled. "It was a mistake and I regret the hell out of it," she said. "Jack did not deserve it and now I have to live with it. But I can assure you that nothing about my relationship with Garret had anything to do with Jack's murder."

Kate knew better than to believe such a blanket statement but still leaned toward Blake being innocent. If it came down to it, basic interrogation and cross-checking of alibis would likely prove it.

"Who else other than Jasmine Brooks might have known?"

"I honestly don't know," she said. "Jasmine was the only person I told. And I don't think Garret told anyone. I asked him not to and he swore that he hadn't. Please...does this have to come out?"

There was something there—maybe a flicker in her eyes or the way she looked away quickly. Something was there...something that made Kate wonder if Missy was being completely truthful.

"No," Kate said. "There's no reason for that. But I hope you can understand that given how everyone—including yourself—told us how great and perfect your marriage was, a hidden affair suddenly has to become our main focus until it's been properly investigated."

Missy nodded but without any real enthusiasm. "With all due respect," she finally said, "I hope you've got the information you need, but I'd really like for you leave now. True...I did this to myself. But I don't need you picking at that one scab..."

Kate stood up, feeling as if she were moving underwater. The tension and angst coming off of Missy was strong—stronger than the thick feeling of loss Kate had felt upon entering the house. As they saw themselves out, a voice called out from the end of the hallway. It startled Kate enough to make her jump slightly.

"Agents?"

Missy was calling out to them. As Kate watched her come back down the hallway toward them, she felt like she was on some weird loop, stuck in a *Groundhog Day* type of scenario.

"I was wondering if you had spoken with Jennifer Nobilini since you'd gotten back into town."

"No. I had considered it, but I didn't see the need in bringing all of that pain back up for her."

"That's considerate."

"Any reason you ask?" DeMarco asked.

"For that very reason. It's a very touchy topic. She fears that's how the town sees her now. The widow with the husband that got shot in the back of the head. I think she gets depressed whenever it comes out in conversation. We may not be best friends by any means, but I do care for her. Just looking out..."

Kate understood that, but she also wondered if Jennifer might still be holding something of a grudge against the FBI not finding her husband's killer eight years ago.

"Do you think you *will* speak with her?"

"I don't know," Kate said. "And if I were, I can't exactly tell you about the details of our investigation when it concerns other people."

Missy nodded, but looked a little put off.

Kate could feel herself growing aggravated. Rather than responding in any way, she simply gave a quick nod and turned away. "Thanks again for your time, Mrs. Tucker," she said. "I know it can't be easy."

When she was outside and headed down the porch steps, she didn't realize that her entire body had gone tense until DeMarco closed the door behind them and caught up with her on the sidewalk.

"You okay?" DeMarco asked.

"Yeah. I just…I still feel like she's hiding something. I think more people might know about the affair. And as of right now, I really do wonder if we should speak to Jennifer Nobilini after all. Damn, I hate this town. I know that's an immature thing to say, but it is what it is."

"She never got answers," DeMarco said. "She probably still needs someone to blame. And without a killer tucked securely behind bars somewhere…"

"I know, I know."

But as they got into the car, DeMarco taking the driving duties this time, Kate's anxiousness slowly faded away and became something else. She thought about Frank Nobilini's murder and how she had come across some of the same obstacles while dealing with that case: a lack of clues, a perfect life with no scratches or rough edges anywhere. Everything about that case had been exactly similar to Jack Tucker's, right down to the way in which they were murdered.

So why would it stop now? If everything had been the same so far, maybe this new development would be the same, too. What if there was some secret affair buried in Jennifer Nobilini's past, too?

Stop painting everyone in this town as an adulterous demon, she told herself. *Just because the seemingly perfect Tucker family had a provocative skeleton in their closet doesn't mean everyone does.*

Still, the discovery of Missy Tucker's affair had thrown her for a loop. And then, when they had gotten here to question her, Missy had specifically asked about Jennifer Nobilini. Given the situation, it did make sense; Jennifer had apparently called her, just checking in on a recent widow who was enduring the same pains and sorrows Jennifer had faced.

True, Kate thought, looking back to the Tucker house as DeMarco pulled away from the curb. *But what if?…*

CHAPTER TWENTY

Kate grabbed the most recent printouts from the printer as DeMarco looked through the handful of sheets that had already been sent through. She looked unconvinced but the tiniest bit excited.

"Okay," DeMarco said. "Explain to me one more time how this isn't a huge assumption."

"I never said it *was* anything other than a huge assumption. But it hit me as we were leaving the Tucker house. Everything about the Nobilini case and the Tucker case have been exactly the same. *Everything.* The way they were murdered, the location the bodies were found, the perfect marriage, a great job, perfect life, same town, and on and on. And now, today, we get this bombshell that Missy Tucker was actively involved in an affair up until not very long prior to her husband's murder. No one expected it or would have thought it could happen. So rather than assume it's the one thing that makes the cases different and being content with that, maybe we need to consider the fact that it might just be yet another similarity in the cases."

"Yes, but you already said that there was no adultery with the Nobilini case."

"I did. And before we spoke with Jasmine Brooks, we didn't think there was any adultery in the Tucker case, either."

"Okay, so what am I looking at?" DeMarco asked. "I see men's names and a few handwritten notes."

"This is a list of the people I spoke to regarding the Nobilini case. The conversations took place over a span of about three months. I think it came down to about twenty-two people."

"So what are we looking for?"

"I think we'd be better served to try to find friends of Frank Nobilini rather than Jennifer. You've seen it yourself so far—people are very hesitant to share dirt on a widow. But if we go after this sort of information under the task of trying to solve a man's murder rather than digging up dirt on his widowed wife, I think we have a better chance of getting information. What we need to do is find a few men on this list that still live around here and that seemed willing to talk openly when the case was still open."

"So we're cold-calling friends of Frank Nobilini's?"

"Pretty much."

DeMarco had no arguments or further questions. Kate felt like she was scrutinizing DeMarco's every move. After her reaction to delivering news of Jack's death to Missy when the case started, she was afraid something similar might happen after the most recent visit. But DeMarco seemed to be taking it all in stride, making no snide comments or acting rude or defensive in any way. She was, though, asking more questions than usual. And Kate was pretty sure she knew why.

"We joked about it before on the phone," Kate said, "but Duran asked you to babysit me, didn't he?"

"More or less. I'm supposed to keep track of your methodology and how you approach the case."

"He thinks I'm slipping in my old age, I take it?"

"No, not at all. He thinks you're as sharp as ever, actually. But—and if you ever tell him I told you this, I'll deny it to the grave and never talk to you again—he thinks that coming

off of retirement and being in this sort of part-time limbo, you're being a little lackluster in adhering to bureau protocol. He didn't use the term *loose cannon,* but that's basically what he was getting at."

"Loose cannon," Kate said with a little laugh. "Hey, I've been called worse."

"And if this case keeps going the way it has," DeMarco said with her own laugh, "I'm sure you'll continue to hear worse."

Kate knew that it was a joke, but it still hurt a bit. Whatever babysitting tasks Duran had tasked DeMarco with, she was taking them seriously. And that was fine with Kate. She had no problem proving to two different people that she still had enough gas in the tank—maybe even enough to not only wrap Jack Tucker's case, but Frank Nobilini's as well.

**

The best man to speak with—who had been the most helpful and insightful when Kate had been in Ashton eight years ago for Frank's murder—was no longer a local. He had taken a job in Iceland and moved his entire family to Reykjavik. That left a handful of other men to visit, none of whom Kate remembered clearly from the Nobilini case.

The first was a man named Robert Jansen. He lived on the same block as the Nobilinis and had a job as an executive banker in Manhattan. That's how they ended up going back into Manhattan,

109

scrambling for a parking space in the hurried post-lunch congestion of Midtown. After grabbing a quick lunch of their own, they paid a visit to one of the largest banks in New York City. The first-floor ceilings were cavernous, all glass and black décor, like some legendary castle with a modern industrial twist.

They checked in at the front lobby desk, greeted by a woman who, as cruel as the judgment seemed, looked like she was *meant* to work at a high-scale bank.

"We need to speak with Robert Jensen," Kate said.

"Of course," the woman said in a rehearsed yet cheerful tone. "I assume you have an appointment."

"No."

"Well," DeMarco said, leaning forward and quickly showing her ID, "we do *now*. This is urgent, ma'am. We need to see him as soon as possible."

The woman was flustered as she got up from the desk and nodded to them. "Oh, yes, of course. Have a seat, ladies. It may take five or ten minutes, but I'll get him for you."

They took a seat and it took Kate less than ten seconds to see that DeMarco was still very antsy. "What is it?" Kate asked.

"I don't want you to think I'm doubting your instincts, but it seems almost like a waste of time to be venturing back to this case. If there were hard evidence, sure, I'd understand. But we're talking to people that you talked to eight years ago—people that even by your description, weren't able to offer help."

"No, that's a legitimate concern. However, I also know that time heals all things. If these people were purposely not sharing dirt on the Nobilinis, the chances are such loyalty might have waned over time. Plus, the fact that we're still asking about it eight years later might clue them in to just how important it is."

DeMarco nodded her head but still did not seem convinced. Kate did not take offense. After all, in the end, it might turn out that DeMarco was right.

It took another six minutes before the woman from the desk reappeared. She was escorting a short plump man down an expansive corridor that led between the check-in desk and the remainder of the bank that sat beyond. The man spotted Kate and DeMarco and came walking over with the kind of caution a man might show as he walked through an active minefield.

There seemed to be a flicker of recognition as he looked to Kate but it was fleeting. He took a seat next to them, leaning in and speaking quietly. "I'm told you're from the FBI?"

"Yes," Kate said.

He looked worried, making Kate wonder if there might be something he was doing here at work that he was afraid might potentially attract the FBI. But she tucked this feeling to the side. She could not allow herself to be distracted by such rabbit trails.

"I don't know if you remember me," Kate said. "I spoke with you about eight years ago after—"

"That's it. I thought you looked familiar! You were the agent looking into Frank Nobilini's murder, right?"

"That's correct. I'm Agent Kate Wise, and this is my partner, Agent DeMarco. We're actually looking back into that case to try to solve a recent murder—another person from Ashton, the body discovered here in the city."

"Oh my God," Jensen said. Clearly, he had not yet heard about Jack Tucker. "Well, what can I do? I'm not sure how I can help."

"In the case notes from the Nobilini murder, I have you down as being rather helpful. You were a friend of Frank's correct?"

"I was, yes. Not *best* friends by any stretch of the imagination, but I knew him well."

"And did you or your wife know Jennifer well?" DeMarco asked.

"Not as well as Frank. Jennifer was the type that was quiet at parties. Always sitting by herself. Not in a rude or isolated way, but she just wasn't as outgoing as Frank."

"But in your opinion, she was good to Frank?" Kate asked.

"God yes. Those two were inseparable. The type that was always holding hands or exchanging little kisses out of nowhere. Really sweet."

"So if I asked you if you thought there was any way she might have been involved in an affair, your reaction would be what?"

"No way. You know, I don't even know if she's dated a single time since Frank died. They were maddeningly in love. Sickeningly so, if I'm being honest." He smiled, as if remembering the two of them together. "They just…they had it together, you know? A lot of other couples in Ashton wanted what they had."

"Given that Ashton is such a small town, I find it hard to believe that not a single negative word was never breathed about either of them," Kate said.

Jensen seemed to be thinking about something, as if his brain and snagged on a particular memory. "If I'm being honest, I don't remember *anything* negative about them while they were alive. But pretty recently—maybe within the last two years, actually—I do remember one thing."

"What was it?"

"I got a promotion here at the bank two years ago. It meant more pay, but also more work. A lot of weekend trips away to Chicago and Dallas in particular. My wife is a stay-at-home mom but she does have a small business that she operates from home so she attends the occasional conference on the weekends here and there. So we looked into hiring someone to help around the house. Not a nanny per se, but more like a housekeeper. We have four kids, so we thought it was necessary. We asked around for good reputable housekeepers and got the names of a few women. We interview three and one of them used to work for the Nobilinis— right around the time they had their first kid, I believe. We asked about her experience and even told her that we had known Frank and Jennifer quite well. She told us about her time there and one of the things she honed in on for highlighting her experience was how she had handled everything in stride and grace in the midst of Frank and Jennifer arguing all the time. This, of course, shocked my wife and I."

"Did she say what the arguments were about?" Kate asked.

"No. She didn't go into detail. But she said it was almost a weekly thing. Sometimes, she said, it would be pretty bad. Honestly, though, that's about as detailed as she got."

"Did you end up hiring her?" DeMarco asked.

"No, we ended up going with someone else and it's worked out well."

"What's the name of the woman that worked for the Nobilinis?" Kate asked.

"Lizzy Trabisky."

"Do you know if she is currently working as a housekeeper in Ashton?"

"Yeah, actually, I think she is. For the Nolan family."

Kate felt a little out of sorts; here she was, elated that they finally found someone who had something negative to say about a murder victim from eight years ago. It was an odd thing to feel triumphant about for sure.

"Thank you, Mr. Jensen," Kate said as she got to her feet.

"Forgive me for asking," Jensen said. "But two murders so similar, eight years apart. Is this something we should worry about? We—as in anyone living in Ashton."

"It's far too early to make such a statement, but based on the span of time between the murders, I would highly doubt it." But even as she gave this answer, she dwelled on the idea for the first time. She started to wonder if there had been other murders in Ashton that might be linked to the Tuckers and Nobilinis but, because they had seemed so common in nature, had not been highlighted.

Stop overcomplicating things, she told herself. *You're already having to reach back into a nearly decade-old case. How much harder do you want to make it on yourself?*

Robert Jensen seemed to take comfort in her answer, though. He gave them a quick and awkward wave goodbye as he headed back to work. Kate and DeMarco headed straight for the door, finally with a promising lead to explore.

As they got into the car, Kate tried to recall how many times they had made the jaunt back and forth between New York City and Ashton, but she had lost count.

Hopefully, she thought as she wound her way through traffic, *this will be the last time.*

CHAPTER TWENTY ONE

It was hard to consider it ironic because Ashton was so small, but the Nolan family lived on the same street as Cass Nobilini, right on the outskirts of Ashton's main hub. It was a very quaint cottage-style house. An honest-to-God tire swing hung from one of the several trees in the side yard, which was separated from the neighboring yard with a beautiful yet cliché white picket fence.

As it turned out, Lizzy Trabisky was much the same as the house: beautiful, but cliché. She looked to be roughly thirty with gorgeous auburn hair and just enough makeup on to highlight her sultry eyes but not be overbearing. She wore a thin spaghetti-strapped tank top that was cut just above the belly button and a pair of yoga pants that were so tight, they may as well have been painted on.

She answered the door with a confused smile. Kate hated herself a bit for her initial reaction of Lizzy. She had never truly believed that people this pretty could be legitimate. She did her best to shove that feeling aside as she and DeMarco introduced themselves.

"Yeah," Lizzy said with feigned sorrow. "I heard about Mr. Tucker a few days ago. It's so terrible. But I don't see how it's the same as what happened to Mr. Nobilini."

"Well, that's what we're working on," DeMarco said. "And in speaking with Robert Jensen, we discovered that you once worked for the Nobilinis. Is that correct?"

"Yes. It was right before he was killed. I think they let me go about four months or so before his body was found."

"Can we come inside and talk it over?" DeMarco asked.

"I'd rather do it on the porch," she said. "One of my duties as the Nolans' housekeeper is to serve as a part-time nanny for their youngest kids. Darcy is three, and she's down for a nap right now."

"That's fine," Kate said.

"Want me to grab some tea or lemonade or something?"

"No thanks. This shouldn't take very long."

Seeming a little disappointed, Lizzy stepped out onto the porch. There were five wicker chairs situated around the porch and each of them took one, right beside one another.

"We wanted to speak to you," Kate said, "because Mr. Jensen said he had interviewed you about a housekeeping job in the past."

"He did. About two years ago, I think it's been."

"During that interview, you spoke a bit about your time working with the Nobilinis. Particularly about some arguments they'd had. Do you remember any of those arguments?"

"Not well, but I *do* remember them arguing quite a bit. I also remember, though, how the Jensens seemed very shocked by that. I think they had this picture-perfect image of the Nobilinis in their mind."

"Was there ever physical abuse?" DeMarco asked.

"No, not that I knew of. Some of the arguments got a little heated, but I'm fairly certain neither of them had the sort of mean streak to actually attack one another."

Kate didn't quite know why, but she was fairly certain Lizzy was lying to them. It was all over her body language and the way she refused to keep her eyes in one place. She had a shitty poker face and, as far as Kate was concerned, it was telling her just about everything she needed to know.

"With all due respect," Kate said, leaning forward in her seat, "I'm going to ask you to please stop lying. I don't know what you're lying about, but I need the truth here. Frank died all those years ago and we never found the killer. And now there's a good chance that he's back, and has killed Jack Tucker. There's a connection somewhere in there and we can't find it because for some reason, no one in this town cares to shed some light on the dark places. I don't know what you're afraid of, Lizzy...but I need you to tell us the truth."

With each few words Kate spoke, she could see a sheen of tears gathering in the corners of Lizzy's eyes. She went tense and there was a single moment when Kate thought she was going to get up from her chair and escape inside.

"Bear in mind," Kate added, "anything you tell us stays with us and, at most, our superiors and local PD. No one in this town has to know anything you tell us."

"I just...God, I just wish I'd never worked for them."

Kate gave her a moment to get a rein on her feelings and then pressed forward. "What was it, Lizzy? What happened?"

She started right away, as if afraid she might lose the nerve. "Well, they were always bickering about something. Money, how to raise the kids, what church to go to on Sundays, things like that. But when they were in public or had people over at the house, it was totally different. They were like this dream couple. But there was one argument that was the worst. I nearly missed it because I was scheduled to leave at six...that was when my job was over for the day. But I was behind on something—I honestly forget what—and was still there around six thirty or so when they started yelling at each other.

"I think what happened was that Frank had found some sort of message on Jennifer's phone...a message from another man. I don't know what it said, but it was enough to make him accuse her of cheating. She blew up on him, asking him how he could dare accuse her of such a thing. I saw that it was getting bad, so I took the kids out into the front yard and drew on the sidewalk with some sidewalk chalk. I caught bits and pieces of the argument from outside. He threatened to take the kids and leave. She dared him to. There was a lot of shouting and then it was just over."

"Did anything at all happen after that?" Kate asked.

"Not with them, no. But Jennifer came outside a few minutes later and told me everything was good and that I could go home. I worked for them for three more days and then they let me go. I don't know for sure if it was because they knew what I'd heard or what...but it's what I have always assumed."

"Did you have any kind of interactions from them after that?"

"No. But it seemed weird to me. They never gave me a straight answer as to why they fired me, but they told me that I could use them as a recommendation for future jobs. And as far as I know, they've done that at least twice."

"What about the kids? Do you see them around anymore?"

"Here and there, just in passing. I don't think they really know anything that happened before their dad died. That's sort of become their world, you know?" She wiped a tear away and looked surprised that she had been crying at all.

"Thank you, Lizzy," Kate said. "I know this was hard for you. But if you don't mind me asking, why were you trying to lie about it?"

She shrugged and looked down to the boards of the porch floor. "I don't know. It seems wrong to remember the dead like that, you know? And I know how this town feels about Jennifer. She's treated with this weird sort of reverence. Everyone loved her before Frank died but then after he was murdered...I don't know. People see her like a saint or something."

Well, that makes the next step in this case a very awkward one, Kate thought. She looked over to DeMarco and the slow expression of despair creeping across her features indicated that she knew where they needed to go next as well.

They had to pay a visit to Jennifer Nobilini.

And they were going to have to ask her—apparently the patron saint of Ashton, New York—about the potential affair she'd had just a few weeks before her husband had been killed.

CHAPTER TWENTY TWO

Jennifer Nobilini looked like she had aged almost twenty years in the past eight. She looked worn down. She still had a slender frame and a well-chiseled face, but she looked perpetually tired and, despite the beaming smile she offered, a little rundown when she answered the door. While she did look surprised to see Kate, it was clear that she recognized her.

"Agent Wise," she said.

"Mrs. Nobilini," Kate said. "I'm flattered that you remembered me."

Jennifer smiled thinly. "Of course I remember. And even if I managed to forget, my mother-in-law was a little taken by your hard work when you were working Frank's case."

Was she? Kate wondered. *Seems to me, she thought for a while that she could do my job better than I could.*

"Would you have a few minutes to spare for us?" Kate asked. "This is my partner, Agent DeMarco."

"Oh, of course. Come on in."

Jennifer seemed almost excited to have them in as she stepped aside and opened the door wider. As Kate walked in, she felt a wave of déjà vu tingling across her skin and through her heart. She'd been somewhat taken off guard by the way she'd felt walking into Cass Nobilini's house a few days ago, but this was something altogether different. This was like literally carving open her memory banks and physically stepping inside.

Jennifer led them into the living room which was exactly the way Kate remembered it. A couch and a loveseat, a television perched over the fireplace. Pictures of their family on the walls. In a few of them, Frank Nobilini peered out at Kate, as if asking her what in the hell was taking so long to find his killer. Afternoon sunlight was coming in through the two living room skylights, making the place feel warm and almost ethereal. Honestly, the entire thing was creeping Kate out. It was far too surreal to be back here, back in this house with this same woman that she had failed all those years ago.

And now she was about to turn this poor woman's life upside down.

Or maybe she's not some "poor woman," Kate thought. *She didn't tell me about any of the arguments Lizzy Trabisky told me about. What else was she hiding from me when I was here eight years ago?*

"Jennifer, forgive the abruptness of the question, but could you maybe tell us why you called Missy Tucker?"

"I heard what happened to Jack. Honestly, I've never really been too close with the Tuckers, but I know them well enough. And when I heard how Jack was killed…it brought it all back to me. And I remembered how I had people that were there for me when Frank died, but no one could fully understand what I was going through—what it was like to know that he had been murdered like that. And I thought I could maybe help ease her through it…as much as I could."

"She did seem appreciative," Kate said.

"I imagine this has to be very strange for you," Jennifer said. "Back in this town again with the same sort of murder. Is it going any better this time around?"

"Well, we *are* finding some clues. And quite frankly, a lot of the leads we're getting are all coming back to your husband. And to you as well."

"Really? How's that?"

Kate knew there was no way to ease the woman into the conversation. She also knew that by simply trying to shock people with information, it was a great way to gauge whether they were lying or not.

"As we were looking into Jack Tucker's case, we found that there were many similarities between the Tuckers and you and Frank. A seemingly perfect couple, very much in love. No one could imagine why *anyone* would want to murder either of these men. Yet it happened. And, to be honest, the more we dug, the more skeletons we uncovered."

"Skeletons?"

Kate had really been hoping that Jennifer would willingly admit to the information. But it seemed she was not going to be so lucky.

"Well, for one, it seems that you and Missy Tucker have more in common than husbands that were murdered in a very particular way."

"Liken what?" Jennifer asked. Her tone and posture made it clear that she was shifting into defensive mode.

"Alleged affairs, for starters."

Jennifer sat up straight, her eyes going wide. She looked not particularly shocked, but *scared*. It was like she'd seen a monster and her brain wasn't sure how to handle the sight.

"And these would be affairs that occurred not too long before the deaths of your husbands. In your case, it's looking like about a month or two. In Missy's it was—"

"Would you care to tell me how in God's name you have come to this insulting conclusion?" Jennifer demanded. She was crying, the tears pushed by both sorrow and anger from the looks of it.

"I can't reveal my sources," Kate said. "But Missy has admitted to hers. She did it almost right away, when we confronted her with it. And with a little more digging, we know that you and Frank had—"

"Don't you *dare* speak his name in that context!"

"Fine," DeMarco said, seemingly happy to take over. "Here are the facts as we know them. In both cases, you and Missy Tucker were cheating on your husbands. Both marriages were seen as these perfect storybook marriages in Ashton. And both of your husbands are dead."

"This is sick," Jennifer said. "How can you even think of accusing me of something like this?"

"We have a pretty good reason," Kate said. "A good witness."

"Fucking Lizzy! It was her, wasn't it?"

"Think what you want," Kate said. "But you've now had about two minutes to refute my claims and you haven't."

Jennifer got to her feet and started pacing. She walked the length of the living room and with each step, Kate felt her feet ready to pounce and give chase if Jennifer tried to make a run for it.

"So what if I did?" Jennifer asked, wiping a tear away. She now stood still, her arms crossed over her chest. "Everyone cheats in these towns. Hell, some of the spouses know about it and don't care. If you were going to accuse people of affairs in this town, everyone would be linked. You'd stay busy for *days*."

"Maybe that's true," Kate said. "But as it stands, you and Missy Tucker are the only ones that have husbands that were killed execution style and discarded in an alleyway in Midtown."

Jennifer took a single step forward and pointed an accusing finger at Kate. "You were a lousy agent back then and you're still terrible at your job. You're here to solve a man's murder and all you can do is prove that two women were involved in affairs. Hey...wow, great work there, Agent Wise."

"Jennifer, I only bring it up to show you that there are connections here that go beyond the murder of your husbands. The affairs…if there are any links within those as well, we might be able to find out who the killer is. And if not *who*, then almost certainly *why*. We just need your cooperation and—"

"We all have ghosts and demons, Agent Wise," Jennifer said. "I am not proud of mine and the timing of my transgressions is unfortunate. But that's something I have to live with every day. I certainly don't need an FBI agent who is apparently terrible at her job throwing it in my face!"

DeMarco got to her feet but remained as calm as she could. "Mrs. Nobilini, your truthfulness can help us find a killer. You could—"

"I want you both out of my house right now," Jennifer said. "And just be warned that I fully intend to file a complaint to the FBI for having two of their agents trying their best to tarnish the reputation of a widow—a widow who has never had full closure over her husband's death due to the negligence of one of their agents. Now *get out!*"

Kate took a few moments to consider her options. She could continue pressing and perhaps hope that Jennifer would crack under the pressure. She had just admitted to an affair, though had given no details. Perhaps the admission of an affair was enough. Because if they now knew the affair had legitimately occurred, there had to be *someone* else who knew about it. Particularly the man that Jennifer Nobilini had been sleeping with.

She finally got to her feet. She did not bother with a thank-you or an apology of any kind. She simply took her leave, with DeMarco trailing behind her. The closer Kate got to the door, the more she realized how much the Nobilini house was making her feel suffocated—as if the past had grown a pair of hands and had them wrapped around her neck.

***

When they were outside and back in the car, Kate wasted no time in cranking the car and pulling away from the curb.

"You think she was bluffing about the call?" DeMarco asked.

"Hard to tell. That woman had so many emotions riding through her…"

"So how in the hell are we supposed to figure out who she was having the affair with?"

"I don't know yet. But think about how we found out about this affair in the first place. We spoke to Lizzy Trabisky. A housekeeper who worked for the Nobilinis. Everyone else had this picture of perfection of them. But it was the housekeeper that knew about the potential affair. Because they work on the inside, if you will."

"And?"

"Well, anytime there's a crime in a suburban neighborhood where there are housekeepers and nannies, they almost always have the best insights. They hear and see a lot that others in the community aren't aware of."

"Lizzy Trabisky already said she didn't know much."

"True. But she's not the only housekeeper in Ashton. And I'm sure there are countless nannies and regular babysitters."

Before DeMarco could respond, a thought occurred to Kate. "Do me a favor, would you? Call Robert Jensen's bank and get him on the phone. He said they interviewed three potential housekeepers, passing on Lizzy Trabisky. Find out who he *did* hire and get her information from him. We'll start with her and work our way down the Ashton grapevine."

Nodding with enthusiasm, DeMarco did as Kate asked. Kate listened as DeMarco spoke with a receptionist, waited patiently for a bit, and then started speaking with Jensen. The conversation was brief and went well. DeMarco seemed pleased when she ended the call.

"He says his housekeeper's name is Tonya Gallahan. She's at their house right now—works Monday through Thursday from eight in the morning until four in the afternoon. If she's not there, Jensen says to wait around a bit; it means she's just not back from picking his older son up from school yet. He said he's going to call ahead and let her know we're on the way."

"Great. Look, I know this might seem like a shot in the dark…"

"No, not at all. I trust you. You've got far more experience than I do." She paused for a moment and added: "Look…yes, Duran has me sort of watching over you. But unless it's something completely reckless, I'm never going to question your approach. This whole case seemed dead and hopeless two days ago. And now I finally feel like it might all be leading somewhere. So please know I see myself more as a partner than…well, a *spy*."

"I appreciate that," Kate said. "Now, can you pull up directions to Jensen's address?"

"He gave it to me on the phone," she said with a smile. "It's only about a mile away."

"God bless a small town," Kate said with a nervous smile.

CHAPTER TWENTY THREE

The timing was perfect. Kate parked her car in front of the Jensen residence just as two kids and a driver climbed out of a black Audi that had just parked in the paved driveway. As Kate and DeMarco got out, the kids looked their way. The youngest—a little boy of about four or so—waved excitedly at them. Kate waved back with a smile. She honestly didn't miss these younger years with children, but she did miss the joy kids seemed to have over everything at that age.

The driver, a young woman with her hair in a ponytail and wearing a New York Giants T-shirt, waved at them as well. This, presumably, was Tonya. "Mr. Jensen said you were coming," she said across the lawn. "Come on in and join the chaos."

Kate and DeMarco accepted the invitation, walking across the perfectly green lawn and to the porch. The little boy held the door open for them. Kate's heart warmed a bit when she watched DeMarco give the boy a fist bump and a smile. The kid smiled right back and then went rushing into the house. The older kid—another boy, around the age of ten or eleven, if Kate had to venture a guess—gave them both a lazy wave as he scrolled through his phone while walking through the door.

Tonya Gallahan came next, nodding into the doorway. "Go on, go on," she said. "I'm always lagging behind. These kids are fast."

They entered the house to the sounds of the youngest boy rummaging in the kitchen for a snack. Tonya led Kate and DeMarco into the kitchen as well. Tonya gave them both a quick *one second* gesture and turned to the kids.

"All right, guys, I need you to be really quiet and do something together for a little while, okay? These are some friends of your dad's and they're here to ask me some important questions."

"Can we play Fortnite?" the young one asked.

"It's too violent for you," the older brother said with great satisfaction. He then sighed and took his brother gently by the arm. "Come on. We can play that dumb game you like."

"Yay! Candyland!"

And with that, both of the boys exited the spacious kitchen, snacks in hand. Tonya looked back to Kate and DeMarco with her eyes wide and a tired smile on her face. "Sorry about that."

"Are you kidding?" DeMarco asked. "They're incredibly well behaved. And you're very good with them."

"Thanks. Yeah, they can be pretty stinking sweet when they want to be."

"Tonya," Kate said, "how long have you worked for the Jensens?"

"Nearly two years now. I started out just as a two-day sort of thing, but when Mrs. Jensen's small business from home picked up, they asked me to come on four days a week."

"Do you enjoy it?"

"Most of the time. I'm twenty-seven and not through with college yet. So it's sort of a means to an end right now."

"Mr. Jensen said he'd call ahead and let you know we were coming," DeMarco said. "Did he tell you why we needed to speak with you?"

Tonya looked out of the kitchen and down the hall to make sure the boys were indeed out of earshot. "Something about Jack Tucker's murder is all I know. He said it was just innocent questions and that I had nothing to worry about."

"And that's exactly correct," Kate said. "However, I have been at this job long enough to know that in small towns like Ashton, babysitters and housekeepers are typically the best source of information when it comes to gossip and dirt. Please forgive the stereotype."

"Oh, no offense taken. Besides…I'd say that's pretty accurate."

"Did you know Jack Tucker at all?"

"No. But I know Missy. I see her from time to time at the school when there are programs and fundraisers."

"And how about Jennifer Nobilini? Do you know her?"

"Only by name. From what I hear, her husband died eight years ago in pretty much the same way Jack Tucker was killed. Is that right?"

"It is," Kate said. "Though we can't provide you with any details. Tonya…the reason we're here is because we do feel that the two murders are connected. And again, while I can't give details, we *have* come to discover that there might be more links to the two murders than we thought. But, as you can imagine, not everyone in Ashton is particularly being honest or forthright with us."

"Yeah, I can believe that."

"I want to know your feelings about Missy Tucker first," Kate said. "Do you know her well enough to give an informed opinion?"

"Not really. All I can say is that she's been nothing but nice to me in the past. And her kids are very polite. They don't really hang out with the Jensen boys, so I don't really know them all that well, either."

"And what about Jennifer Nobilini?"

"Like I said, I don't know her. So any opinion I have wouldn't be based on much."

"What about rumors?" DeMarco asked. "Have you heard anything about her or her lifestyle either before are after her husband was murdered eight years ago?"

Tonya shook her head. "No. I think she's sort of untouchable around here. After her husband's murder and everything, people kind of really respect her."

"So you've heard nothing about her?" Kate asked. "Maybe about her and a romantic relationship with someone?"

"No. Sorry."

"Have you heard her name mentioned at all in the last few months?"

"No. I can't…wait. Yes, actually. Oh my God. Okay, so last Wednesday when I went to pick Owen up at school…there was this sort of commotion at the top of the car rider line. I was about a dozen cars deep, so I didn't see it all. But the whispers and gossip spread down the line quick. There was someone there to get the Nobilini kids, but it wasn't Jennifer. And that was strange because Jennifer *always* picks her kids up from school. She's usually among the last of the parents to swing through the car rider line, but she's always there."

"Who was trying to pick them up?" Kate asked.

"I don't know. I never heard a name. Just some man. The woman in the car in front of me said he looked creepy and was getting sort of verbal with one of the teachers manning the car rider line."

"Did the police get involved?" DeMarco asked.

"I don't think so. Before things got too heated, the guy just left. From what I understand, nothing was ever done about it. But really, that's all I know."

Some guy shows up and tries to pick up the Nobilini kids sometime very soon before Jack Tucker was killed, Kate thought. *What the hell is going on?*

"I'm sorry I can't be more help," Tonya said.

"Oh, this is a huge help," Kate said. "Tonya, thank you so much for your time. And if you can keep these questions between just the three of us, that would be greatly appreciated."

"Sure, of course."

Tonya walked them back to the front door. Kate could hear the boys giggling, playing Candyland somewhere down the house's main hallway. Outside, the day was cooling a bit as the afternoon wound down. Kate knew they had received a lot of information today and had constantly been on the move, but she didn't realize so much of the day had escaped them.

As they got back into the car for what felt like the hundredth time, Kate looked over to DeMarco and asked: "Feel like going back to the elementary school?"

"You thinking maybe they caught the guy on the security cameras?"

"That's the hope."

As Kate sped away from the Jensen residence and back out into Ashton, DeMarco got on the phone and called the school, ensuring someone would be there after hours. Kate meanwhile was still stuck on the puzzle that had come to her while speaking with Tonya.

Jack Tucker is murdered in the same way as Frank Nobilini; it's discovered that Jennifer Nobilini and Missy Tucker were both having affairs that took place within a few months of their husbands' murders; while the Tucker case is active, a strange man tries to pick the Nobilini kids up from school.

Just what in the hell is going on?

Kate wasn't sure yet, but as they neared the school and she kept going through that chain of information in her head, she certainly felt like they were finally headed toward some definitive answers.

CHAPTER TWENTY FOUR

Most of the faculty and staff had left for the day by the time Kate and DeMarco arrived at Ashton Elementary at 5:04 that afternoon. The only staff remaining in the office was the vice principal and the school nurse. The art teacher was also running around in and out of the office, preparing for an art show the next day. She was making copies in the office copy room while Kate and DeMarco waited for the vice principal to come up front.

"That's some impressive work," DeMarco said, pointing to a photocopy of a black and white sketch.

"Oh, thank you," the art teacher said. "There's going to be a lot of fantastic work at our show tomorrow. Are you parents of students here?"

"No," DeMarco said. "Just visiting."

"That's a shame. It's going to be a great show. The pieces are even going to be auctioned off. Nothing huge, of course. Fun little bids that will go to local charities. Something the PTA set up. It was a nice touch, I thought."

"That sounds wonderful," Kate said.

"Well, if you can't make it tomorrow, feel free to swing by the gymnasium and look at some of the work I've already put up. The kids here are quite talented."

"I doubt we'll have time, but thanks all the same," DeMarco said. "And good luck with the show tomorrow."

The art teacher grabbed up the last of her copies and dashed back out the door. As she did, the vice principal finally made her way to the front desk. She was a tall older woman who introduced herself as Mrs. Talley. She showed the agents the monitor that sat behind the check-in desk, showing three different angles around the school: the front parking lot, the rear parking lot, and the central playground sitting on the western edge of the property.

"Of course, this is all live feed," Mrs. Talley said. "Anything we need to do to enhance or review the footage needs to be done from the central console. I'm not the best with it, but I can probably do enough to get you what you need."

She then led them from the front part of the office toward the back. They passed a few staff offices, the nurse's office, and then came to a small filing room. Sitting against the front wall was a small table with a relatively new security hub on it.

"When I got your call, I took the liberty of pulling up the afternoon in question, but I haven't had a chance to scroll through it yet."

"Do you mind?" DeMarco asked, sitting down behind the monitors.

Kate wasn't sure if DeMarco was asking her permission or Mrs. Talley's. Kate nodded just in case, while Mrs. Talley said, "Of course."

While DeMarco started to look through the footage, Kate did her best to get a better understanding of what happened.

"Mrs. Talley, were you outside when this all occurred?"

"No, I was in the office. But I got a very detailed report from the teachers that were there. You see, over time, we start to notice trends in the arrival of the parents. There are a few that are always first in line to get their kids at the end of the day, and there are a handful that are almost guaranteed to be last. Jennifer Nobilini is nearly always in the last ten cars or so."

"How long does the dismissal process go on for car-riders?"

"Usually about twenty minutes or so. We have a crossing guard up on the main road, and that helps a lot. It's very thorough and efficient."

"And how are the kids let out?"

"Well, that's one of the nice things about living in a smaller town. Many of our teachers know the child by the car that is waiting on them. The children remain on the sidewalk or breezeway, a good distance from the parking lot, while the cars cycle through."

As she explained it, Kate could also see it on the screens. There were roughly twenty kids lined up, waiting for their rides. Many others were behind them, back closer toward the school. She watched as three kids were motioned forward by a teacher standing at the edge of the sidewalk and then watching them as they entered the cars of their parents.

"Right there," Mrs. Talley said, pointing to a red car at the start of the car rider line. "That's the man."

"How long into the dismissal process is this?" Kate asked.

"About four minutes," DeMarco said, pointing to the elapsed time in the bottom corner of the screen.

The three women watched as one of the teachers started to engage with the man in the car. The teacher spoke to him and then looked back behind her—for the Nobilini kids or for more support, it was impossible to tell.

128

They watched the scene in real time. About fifteen seconds later, the man actually opened the door and started to get out.

"That right there," Mrs. Talley said, "proves that he's not accustomed to the car rider line. At the beginning of the year, we send out a notice for all parents to please remain in their car unless there is some sort of emergency or, in the mornings, if their child needs help getting out of the car. So this was the second red flag...the first, of course, being that the two teachers that saw him did not recognize him."

They watched as the man got out and pointed at one of the teachers. When he realized that he was making a scene and that there were impatient parents behind him, he gave up, got in his car, and sped off. The license plate was in view for only a moment; it was blocked by either other cars or out of the screen at almost every moment the car was visible.

"DeMarco, can you back the footage up and zoom in on the man?" Kate asked.

"Yeah, one sec."

DeMarco worked quick, making it evident that she was very well trained on newer systems. The footage reeled backward and when the man was back to standing outside of his car, tuned toward the teachers on the sidewalk, DeMarco froze the footage. She zoomed in slowly and by the time the man became more than just a vague shape on the screen, a hard lump formed in Kate's throat.

"Oh my God," she said.

"What?" DeMarco asked. "Who is it?"

She looked closer, making sure it was not simply her eyes playing tricks on her. It took a second or two for her to be absolutely certain.

"That's Zeus Beringer."

***

"How in the hell is that even possible?" DeMarco asked as they exited the school. "If this guy had plans to kill Jack Tucker within the next day or so, why would he be here trying to pick up the Nobilini kids?"

"I don't know," Kate said. "It doesn't make sense."

But even as she said that, she thought she felt a connection being formed in the back of her mind. She'd been looking for a connection and here it was, practically slapping her in the face. But what did it actually *mean*?

They had gotten back into the car, Kate thinking it might be a good idea to go to the precinct to dig up everything they could on Zeus Beringer outside of his basic criminal record, when her cell phone rang. When she saw Duran's name on the display, she winced. Nine times out of ten, when his name popped up on her cell display, it was bad news.

She answered it, determined not to let whatever bad news he had derail the progress they were making on this case.

"This is Wise."

"Agent Wise, I just got off of the phone with a very irate Jennifer Nobilini. Would you care to tell me how accusing her of an affair has *anything* to do with Jack Tucker's case?"

"Sir, it's where the trail led us. More than that, her affair—"

"*Alleged* affair," Duran interrupted.

"—it adds yet another link between Tucker and Nobilini. It turns out that Missy Tucker was also having an affair during the time leading up to Jack's murder."

"That seems very coincidental. Besides…I still don't see what affairs have to do with these murders. On the surface, it looks like you're doing nothing but digging up dirt on these widows and I shouldn't have to tell you how damning that is for the bureau!"

"I know it all seems like a stretch, but these bits of unfortunate information have given us perhaps the strongest lead in the case." She went on to tell him about the security footage they had just watched—how the man she'd found dead in a Bronx Comfort Inn had showed up at Ashton Elementary in an attempt to pick up Jennifer Nobilini's kids.

The moments of silence after her explanation told her right away that she had Duran hooked. He, too, knew there was something there.

"You may be right, Wise. But if I'm being honest with you, this…well, this case has been eye-opening for me and shows me that we might have made a mistake. I want you back in DC tomorrow. And when you get here, be prepared to hand in your badge. Have DeMarco keep working on the case. But I can't have you on it."

"What? But you—"

But Duran had already ended the call. Kate stared at her phone for a moment and then set it down slowly.

"He's pissed, huh?" DeMarco said.

"Yeah."

"What did he say?"

She thought about not telling her any of it—of telling her it was just a slap on the wrist and that they could carry on as usual. But she could not put DeMarco in that position. God only knew how much trouble she could get in. Besides, she was sure Duran would inform DeMarco soon enough, just to make sure Kate didn't interfere.

"He said the case is yours now. He wants me back in DC by tomorrow. Jennifer Nobilini wasn't bluffing. She called and filed a complaint." She decided to leave out the part where Duran had told her that she would be handing in her badge when she reported back to DC. There was no sense in placing that thought in DeMarco's mind while they worked to finally wrap this damned case.

She thought of Zeus Beringer as they headed back to the precinct. She thought of his sparse apartment and the lack of any real results that had been pulled from his laptop. Sure, Pritchard had found the dark web software, but, as he had said, that really didn't prove much of anything.

But the Ruger found in the motel room seemed to tie it all together.

It was, quite literally, the smoking gun.

And Kate thought that if they could find who had pulled the trigger on Zeus, it would wrap the entire case. And it would be all the better if she could find out before she headed back to DC.

CHAPTER TWENTY FIVE

It was a special sort of hell for Kate to be sitting in her hotel room at 7 o'clock that afternoon, knowing that DeMarco was hard at work down at the precinct. They had parted ways rather awkwardly; it had been clear DeMarco wanted Kate to remain by her side but Kate also knew what was going through the younger agent's head. This was her opportunity to show Duran that she respected him and his orders—and a chance to prove that she could close a case like this one on her own.

She sat on the bed, eating a takeout pizza and staring at the TV, though not watching it. Her mind was still wrapped tightly around the case. She felt a little bit like a villain, but she was trying to figure out a way to wrap the case even without her official FBI capacity. In the end, if she was successful, she'd have to blow her own cover—would have to rely on her position as an agent. Besides—Duran had said she'd have to hand her badge in when she got back to DC. That *technically* meant she was still an active agent. She would not be considered inactive until that badge and ID went across Duran's desk.

She didn't know how rigid Duran was going to be on this, so that meant she could not risk accessing the bureau's network remotely. If he wanted, he could check in on her to see if she had accessed it. That left her with only the scant notes she had on the case that had been printed out. She laid the information she had on Zeus Beringer and Jennifer Nobilini side by side, trying to figure out how the two were connected.

At first glance, it made no real sense. And because of that, Kate let her mind go where it wanted to naturally go. It meant making some assumptions, but she was fine with that for now.

Based on the little bit of evidence at her disposal, she was fine making the assumption that Zeus Beringer had killed at least one of the men she was looking into—probably both of them. The gun in his motel room as well as his reputation among a small group of hitmen seemed to point in that direction. And now that he was dead, that made the *who* question just about obsolete.

There were, of course, a few questions that remained. Why did he kill them? And why was he trying to pick up Jennifer Nobilini's children from school?

She stated to put a theory together—one that made little sense at first but grew more and more appealing the more she thought about it. There was one piece that didn't quite fit, though. And even if she *did* feel comfortable using the bureau network, she wouldn't be able to find the information she needed there anyway.

Her mind kept going back to Jennifer Nobilini and how she had managed to keep her affair mostly quiet. And even after she had more or less admitted to it in front of Kate and DeMarco, there still seemed like she had been hiding something. The fact that she had called Missy Tucker when she barely knew her, even if they did share a similar tragedy, was quite strange, too.

She's hiding something, but what?

Kate considered calling DeMarco to share her theory but thought better of it. DeMarco deserved to be holding the reins of a case. And the last thing she wanted was for DeMarco to feel as if Kate was trying to steal it from her—especially after Duran had removed her from the case.

She had driven to the city this last time so she didn't have to bother with booking a flight. This probably meant that Duran would expect her to drive to DC tonight or, at the very latest, early tomorrow morning. She started to wonder just how late she could leave tomorrow without attracting attention to herself.

While she was thinking, a thought suddenly occurred to her. She recalled their visit to Ashton Elementary that afternoon. She remembered the art teacher, working frantically to get a little fundraising exhibit set up for tomorrow. Hadn't she said something about how the PTA had set the event up?

With a new idea hatching in the back of her head, Kate pulled out her laptop and Googled Ashton Elementary. She went to the website, clicked on the events link, and started to read. The first event, as they were listed in order of scheduled dates, was the art show tomorrow. It was being called The Art Auction Extraordinaire and boasted *"more than fifty art pieces from our very talented fourth and fifth graders."* It was scheduled to start at 8:45 a.m., in the Ashton Elementary gymnasium.

Then, at the bottom of the event information, Kate came across something that all but verified that she was on the right track—that she might be destined to wrap these two cases after all. The last thing listed on the event listing was: *For more information and details about this exciting event, contact Jennifer Nobilini or Alice Delgado.*

Their numbers and email addresses were then given, but Kate had no interest in either of them. She read over the information again with a nervous smile crossing her face.

She already had a plan in mind. Duran had stripped her away from the case. That meant she could get in some very big trouble if she visited a private residence—for instance, paying another visit to Jennifer Nobilini. Besides...she wasn't sure what a visit would really accomplish at this point.

But this art show...well that was open to the public. It was a loophole that would benefit her in the long run, albeit one that Duran could potentially use as a noose to hang her from.

But it was a chance she was willing to take. Because if Duran was already planning on taking her badge, what else did she have to lose? This was yet another thing she thought age was making easier for her—not giving too much of a damn what people, particularly Duran, thought about her.

**

She'd set her alarm for 6:30 the following morning, but she was jerked awake by her cellphone at 6:16 instead. She saw that it was DeMarco and answered it right away, hoping there had been a break in the case. For a moment, she even dared to hope that at some point in the night, DeMarco had managed to find the one missing piece and blown the case wide open.

"Hey, DeMarco."

"Good morning. How are you doing?"

"Jaded. Bummed. Not wanting to drive back to DC today. How about you?"

"Good. Look, we dug up everything on Zeus Beringer last night and there's nothing new. We did see where his name came up in a few other cases—guys that were hired to kill. We're going to revisit some of those cases today—maybe even visit a few in jail to see if we can get more information."

"Good idea," Kate said. She meant it. But she also wasn't going to tell DeMarco about the potentially reckless thing she had planned for the morning. She wasn't going to tell her how she was planning to visit the school and corner Jennifer Nobilini during the art auction—in a place where there would be multiple witnesses if Jennifer tried to get away from her. A place where she would have to remain civil.

DeMarco would almost *have* to report it to Duran and if she did, that would be the end of it. She hated to keep such a secret from DeMarco. When all was said and done, DeMarco would probably be pissed at her for sneaking around behind her back.

But she was willing to risk that.

"I just wanted to wish you well," DeMarco said. "I hate that you were taken off of this. I really do. If it makes you feel any better, Duran chewed me out later on last night. Said I had no backbone and that you apparently swayed me."

"Well, I can sway with the best of them."

"Seriously, Kate. You okay?"

"Yeah, I'm good. It's not the first time I've irritated my superiors."

"You need anything from me before you head back?"

This question hurt a bit. It made Kate all but certain that DeMarco had only made this call to check in on her—to see when she planned on following Duran's orders and heading back.

Makes us even, I guess, she thought. *Given what I plan to do in the next few hours, her little ruse is barely an offense.*

"No, I'm good. I'm going to get dressed, grab some breakfast, and then I'm out of here. How about you? You good?"

"Yeah, I think so. Thanks for getting me this far."

"Sure thing."

They ended the call, Kate riddled with an odd sort of guilt. She nearly called DeMarco back to tell her what she had planned. But that would go one of two ways; either DeMarco would turn her in or she'd go along with it and then she, too, would be reprimanded. So she left the phone where it was as she climbed out of bed and got ready for the morning—a morning that was already starting to feel tense and filled with a sense of finality.

***

When Kate pulled into an empty parking spot at Ashton Elementary school, the last of the school buses had parked in the rear lot, having delivered the last round of students. She headed for the entrance and saw several parents and other adults stepping into the double doors where they were then asked to sign in and have their driver's licenses scanned.

As Kate neared the station to scan her license, she knew this could come back to bite her. But then again, if Duran was going to take her badge, effectively ending this little second career she was compiling, she figured it didn't really matter.

The woman at the scanning station asked her to sign in while she scanned Kate's license. She then looked to Kate with a smile and said: "Are you a parent of a child here?"

"No," she said. "Just visiting. I was here yesterday on business and heard about the auction. I thought it might be a fun way to spend the morning."

"Ah, I see. Well, you certainly aren't the only non-parent here. We've got quite the turnout today. It should be quite the special event! Now, the artwork is already up, but the students won't be in the gym until nine."

The woman then handed her a stick-like name tag that came out of a small mobile printer at the back of the little station.

"Thanks." Kate picked up a nearby flyer for the show and, with an adhesive name tag on her chest, walked into the school for the second time in about fourteen hours.

She followed the small group of adults through the central area of the school and into the gymnasium. However, before she walked into the gym, Kate stepped to the side of the doors and pretended to be looking over the flyer. She peered quickly over it and checked out the inside of the gym. There were many well-designed wooden boards, boasting ten to twelve pieces of art. There were simple sketches and rather elaborate paintings as well. Some of them did indeed look quite nice.

But she wasn't concerned with the artwork. Instead, she glanced around the edges, against the gym's walls. And there, stationed in a corner with a fold-out desk and a steel folding chair, was Jennifer Nobilini. She was speaking to someone standing nearby while also typing something into a laptop. Seeing the laptop, Kate realized that her morning had gotten significantly better.

If that's her laptop, this is going to be much easier than I had thought, Kate thought.

She checked her watch for the time and saw that it was 8:41. The events page on the school website had the auction schedule for 8:45, and the woman at the check-in station said students would be arriving in the gym at 9:00. That was a lot of moving parts and would mean lots of people in and out of the gym, plenty of witnesses to see her if she approached Jennifer and things got heated—which she was certain they would.

She kept the flyer in her hand, making sure she blended in and didn't look suspicious. She eyed the surrounding area, getting a grip on the scene. Adults were still filing in for the art exhibit. The women in the main office, visible through the large picture window that allowed them to see out into the hallway, were chatting and getting ready for another school day. A lone janitor was pushing a large trash can along on wheels, smiling at a passing parent.

And that's when she saw her opening. Right there, between the gymnasium doors and the space where the janitor was standing. She walked slowly in that direction, cautious as she was now out of the throng of adults. She kept the flyer in her hands, pretending to read it as she positioned herself directly in front of the fire alarm on the wall.

She checked quickly to make sure the janitor was not looking at her and there were no teachers or staff looking out of the large office window. When she was certain there were no eyes on her, she reached up and pulled the handle down.

There was a very brief silence between the time she pulled it and the moment the alarm started to blare. She took a single large stride away from it and started to look around in confusion, relying on her rather weak acting skills. Fortunately, she didn't have to rely on them for very long. Within seconds, the adults who had filed into the gym came out in a quick yet organized line. Those that were in the process of coming into the school and headed into the gym were rerouted back the way they had come. Over the din of human movement and a few teachers in the hallways directing people where to go, the alarm blared on.

About ten seconds later, the classrooms started to empty out. Some children were laughing while others were clearly a little frightened. Their teachers led them out of the exits calmly and without much fuss.

Through it all, Kate kept her eyes on the gymnasium doors. She watched the people file out until she caught sight of Jennifer. She was speaking hurriedly to someone in the throng of people, her eyes set dead ahead toward the exit. When Jennifer had passed by within several feet, Kate darted through the crowd of people, the only person heading *toward* the gym rather than away from it.

There were only a handful of people still working their way out of the gym when Kate entered. She figured her best bet was to appear as if she had been there the entire time. She ran toward the back of the gym to where Jennifer Nobilini's little station had been set up. She saw that in her haste, Jennifer had not done anything to protect her computer. Her screen was just it was when she had left it. Currently, there was a document up with a listings of children's names and their artwork, next to empty slots with the headings AUCTIONED FOR and PURCHASED BY.

Kate minimized the document and found that the internet browser was already opened. Kate wasn't at all sure what she was looking for, but she figured she'd know it when she saw it. She hoped maybe her email would be up and already logged into, but there was no such luck there. The browser's window was blank, opened up to the basic Google home page. Thinking quickly, Kate pulled up Jennifer's browsing history. She could tell right away that she was not the type who cleaned it out often; there appeared to be several weeks of online activity still listed under her basic history log.

Shew scrolled through it all, scanning each entry. There were lots of email log-ins and Pinterest pages but nothing of any real substance. That was, until she came to a Craigslist listing. She recalled Alvin Carpenter mentioning that some hitmen would use Craigslist for their business, either posting clever and subtle ads or waiting for clients to post ads.

She opened up the page and found a very brief listing. Only, it was not an ad that she had responded to, but one she had posted. The ad had been posted thirteen days ago and was posted under Relationships. The listing title was **Tired of My Husband.** All the ad said was: *Tired of my husband. Seeking a man with a keen eye for detail and can get the job done.*

It was an alarming ad for sure, but Kate was more confused than anything else. Frank had been killed eight years ago. Why would she post something like this last week? It was a clever ad, especially if it was meant for someone in particular. There was a certain provocative tone to the wording but someone who was looking for something non-sexual could certainly see something else as well.

A keen eye...

...can get the job done.

And it had been posted last week.

The theory she had been stitching together in her head since last night suddenly all fell into place. It was like being overcome with an epiphany or a moment of clarity. She knew that anything she did from this point on would be scrutinized by Duran and would likely result in the end of any hope she had of reconciliation with the bureau. But she also could not let this go. She could call DeMarco, sure, but there was no guarantee that DeMarco would go with her hunch—especially not if Duran had already instructed her to cut Kate out of the case.

"Shit," Kate breathed, and ran back out of the gymnasium. She fell in at the back of the line that was even still meandering out of the school and out toward the rear parking lot.

From what she could tell, this exit had only been for those in the gym and the front office. It appeared that the kids and the teachers had taken an exit on the opposite side of the school. Kate could hear some excited chatter from the other side of the building, mixed with the still-blaring alarm. There was no real sense of panic among the adults. It was as if everyone knew that there was no real threat here. Still, there was just enough commotion for Kate to blend in with everyone else. She used that advantage to scan the crowd for Jennifer Nobilini.

It took her about twenty seconds to locate Jennifer in the crowd of seventy-five or so people. She slowly made her way over, coming in at an angle so that Jennifer wouldn't see her and try to make an escape. She made her way through the crowd with a few simple *excuse me* statements and managed to come up directly behind Jennifer.

"Mrs. Nobilini..."

Jennifer turned around. When she saw Kate, she recoiled a bit, as if she had been slapped. "What the hell are you doing here?"

"I know what you did," Kate said. This wasn't one hundred percent true, but she felt that she knew enough to do what she was about to do.

"You made that perfectly clear yesterday," Jennifer spat. "What the hell are you doing here? Trying to publicly embarrass me?"

"I'd prefer not to do that. It would be much easier if you came peacefully with me. Mrs. Nobilini, I'm placing you under arrest."

"Are you fucking kidding me?" She said this loud enough for a few people around them to take notice.

Kate leaned closer and said, "I know about the Craigslist ad."

Again, Jennifer looked like someone had reached out and slapped her. It was more than enough of a reaction to tell Kate that was indeed some kind of guilt there.

"I'm placing you under arrest. You can come with me peacefully or I can handcuff you right here in front of everyone. Your choice."

"I complained about you yesterday," Jennifer said. "And I was told explicitly that it would be handled. I have a feeling you arresting me without hard proof is going to be bad for you."

"I'm willing to take that chance. Again, it's your choice, Mrs. Nobilini."

Kate could have never expected what happened next. Jennifer Nobilini tried to slap her. It came fast but with great inexperience. Kate caught the slap easily, then twisted the arm so sharply that it caused Jennifer to twist her body around. She yelled out in pain—

whether out of actual pain or just attract attention in the hopes of generating some bullshit brutality charge, Kate wasn't sure. Whatever the reason, it made it that much easier for Kate to slap the set of handcuffs that she had been hiding under her jacket onto Jennifer's wrists.

There were a few gasps but the crowd had fallen mostly silent. The fire alarm continued to blare behind Kate as she pushed Jennifer Nobilini along toward her car. She roughly placed Jennifer in the back of the car and locked the door. Before she got behind the wheel, though, Kate knew there was one other thing she had to do…something she was not looking forward to.

She took out her cell phone and placed a call to DeMarco.

When DeMarco answered, Kate took a breath and said: "I did something you aren't going to like very much. Can you meet me at the precinct in half an hour?"

CHAPTER **TWENTY SIX**

One thing Kate had not been prepared for was for the NYPD to also know that she had been removed from the Jack Tucker case. When she arrived at the precinct and tried to take Jennifer Nobilini inside, she was met with resistance from several of the officers. She made it no farther than the lobby before she was stopped.

"Agent Wise, we can't let you process this woman," one of the officers said. "And we won't do it for you. We know that you've been removed and—"

"Jesus, Kate!"

This was DeMarco's voice, coming from the hallway beyond the bullpen. She was glaring at her from across the bullpen, her eyes filled with fire.

"DeMarco, you need to hear me out."

DeMarco walked up to her, standing face to face. She was acutely aware of the staring officers, but was trying to save face for both of them.

"You should be on the way to DC."

"I should. But something didn't feel right. And I couldn't send you on to seek out my theories out of fear of Duran getting upset."

"You'll be fired for this," DeMarco said sadly.

"Probably."

"You have a good reason for having a handcuffed Jennifer Nobilini?"

Jennifer answered first, bucking against Kate and shouting, "No, she doesn't."

"Yes," Kate said. "DeMarco, give me five minutes to tell you everything I learned this morning...my theory and how I think this all played out."

She could tell DeMarco was at war—part of her wanting to show Duran that she could handle this by herself and was a good babysitter when it came to Kate, and another part knowing that Kate tended to do her best thinking when under pressure.

"Five minutes," she said. "Officer Stephens, can you please take Mrs. Nobilini to a private room for five minutes."

"Sure. Should I uncuff her?"

"Yes. But don't let her leave. Not yet."

DeMarco led Kate back down the hallway, to the small office that had been given to Kate four days ago. As they reached the room, Kate's cell phone started to ring. She knew it would be Duran before she even saw his name on the display.

"You told him what I did?" Kate asked.

"I had to," DeMarco said, closing the door behind them. "You may not give a shit about losing *your* job, but I need mine."

It was a good point and honestly, Kate didn't blame her. She answered the call, fully prepared to catch an absolute nuking from Duran.

"This is Agent Wise," she answered.

"You can drop the *agent* part from your name as of this very second," Duran said. "Kate, listen to me. I respect you and I would be an idiot if I was blind to the amazing career you've had. And for that reason, I am not going to publicly fire you. Rather, I don't want to. But if you so much as look at Jennifer Nobilini in a harsh way, I'll fire you. I'll make a fucking *proclamation* of it if I have to. You blatantly disobeyed me and then you arrested a woman that was never given the relief of having her husband's killer found. What in God's name were you thinking?"

"That's just it," Kate said. "I think I do know who the killer is. For both Frank Nobilini *and* Jack Tucker. Sir, can I put you on speaker to explain this to you and Agent DeMarco at the same time?"

"Make it quick. And let me make this abundantly clear one more time: your reputation is very likely on the line here."

She placed the call on speaker and set it down on the table that DeMarco had claimed as her own over the last twelve hours or so. DeMarco was looking at her with a sense of distrust—and honestly, Kate didn't blame her. She probably felt hurt or even stabbed in the back. If there was to be any future between them, Kate knew an apology would be in order very soon.

Kate did her best to explain her theory…and all of the interlocking pieces that supported it. "A nanny that once worked for the Nobilinis is the only person I have spoken to that claims to have witnessed a less that perfect version of them. Arguing all the time, to the point that one night, Frank threatened to take the kids and leave. He'd found suspicious texts and confronted her about it. I went back to Jennifer and confronted her about it—asking why she lied to us. And she never denied—she basically admitted that yes, she was involved in an affair right around the time of Frank's death. Now this morning, I was able to look at her computer."

"How did you manage to do that?" Duran asked.

She was not at all proud of herself as she walked them through the morning's events. Duran let loose a few expletives from his end of the phone. But he went quiet when she explained the link she had found to the Craigslist ad.

"That's one of the methods your friend Alvin Carpenter said he's known other hitmen to use, right?"

"Right. It's almost like speaking in code."

"Well then how would she know how to reach out to him?" DeMarco asked. "And why?"

"I think she hired Zeus Beringer eight years ago to kill her husband. Frank was threatening to leave her and take the kids—making for an ugly scene. Something that Jennifer Nobilini wasn't willing to risk."

"Okay," Duran said. "Even if I was willing to buy that—and I'm not saying that I am just yet, what about Jack Tucker?"

"I'm not absolutely sure yet, but I have a theory. Director...all I ask is one more chance to speak with her."

"Absolutely not. You're already in enough trouble because of her as it is."

"You're right. But you know how interrogations work. Who is she going to get more defensive with? Who is she most likely to accidentally let something slip with? A woman she loathes or a brand new agent that she's barely spoken to?"

There was a moment of silence—a moment in which DeMarco gave her a pained look. She could sense where this was headed. She could sense that this case, in a few moments, would no longer be hers to run.

"You're right," he said. "But for right now, let DeMarco and this Detective Pritchard fellow tackle it. You can stay there for now as support *only*. But I'm not sending you in there unless it's an absolute last resort."

"Okay," she said. She was surprised and a little deflated; she had been certain Duran would allow her to speak with Jennifer. *Or maybe you're just thinking a little too highly of yourself,* she thought.

She ended the call and looked to DeMarco. "I'm sorry," she said. "But I couldn't let this go. It wasn't because I didn't think you could handle it...I just—"

"I know. It still isn't the best feeling." She sighed and nodded toward the door. "Detective Pritchard is in the conference room with some of the cops. I'm sure they'd appreciate the help."

It was a blow to her ego but she said nothing about it. She simply nodded and took her leave, locating the conference room. Before she could step inside, though, Pritchard was heading out.

"Agent Wise," he said, "I'll skip the pleasantries and just say that I'm sorry to hear about the hot water you're in."

"Yeah, me too. Is there anything I can do to help while Jennifer Nobilini is being interrogated?"

"I'm on the way out to the school to get her computer right now. You're welcome to ride along. Things here are going to get a little heated. Nobilini has already reached out to her lawyer—and she's got a good one. So honestly, unless we can prove something in the next day or so, she's not only going to walk, but she's also talking about suing you and the bureau as well. And if we can't find anything on the computer, she may be able to walk as soon as this afternoon."

"Yeah, then let's go get that computer."

CHAPTER TWENTY SEVEN

It was obvious that Pritchard felt a little awkward to have her riding along with him. They both tried to break the ice with both small talk and pertinent details about the case, but it all fell flat. It then occurred to her that because of her inability to let things go, she had placed herself and the bureau in a fairly bad situation. And now she was left with about a day—if that—to clean up her mess.

When they arrived at the school to pick the laptop up, things had resumed as normal. The art exhibit was finishing up. Parents were leaving the school with art pieces proudly tucked under their arms. Kids had all gone back to their classes and the office was business as usual.

When they got back out to the car, Pritchard walked toward the passenger side. "You mind driving? There's not much I can pull off of this thing without certain software, but I might be able to find a few things."

"No, that's fine."

She got behind the wheel and, for the second time that morning, exited the Ashton Elementary parking lot. As she got onto the main road, she kept track of what Pritchard was doing. She watched from the corner of her eye as he went into his phone's settings, cut on the feature to use it as a Wi-Fi hotspot, and then used it to get Jennifer's laptop online.

He did the same thing Kate had done, going to the internet history and looking around. "Well, if she *was* up to something, she's not very stealthy about it. There's at least three weeks of internet history right here."

He located the ad she had found and read it out loud. "Yeah, that doesn't sound good. But what I don't get...well, her husband died eight years ago. Why is she talking about her husband in this ad?"

Kate almost said *I don't know.* But she was starting to have a good idea. Not one that she was quite willing to share just yet, though.

A few minutes later, Pritchard let out a small *hmmm* sound. "She went to a banking website a day later. And there's no other occurrence within this three-week span that she visited the site. So she's not big on online banking apparently. Just this one occurrence, right after the ad."

"Could we call the bank and get her information?" Kate asked. "I could but, as you know, I don't really have those privileges right now."

"I'll call Agent DeMarco. I'd let the PD handle it but when it comes to banking and getting people's personal info, us lowly detectives and cops don't have the same pull as FBI agents. Depending on who you speak with, they may ask for a warrant."

"Then let's get it. As quickly as possible."

He did it right there and then, calling up DeMarco while Kate drove. It made her feel useless but she also knew that she should really just be glad that Duran hadn't completely yanked her off of the case this morning. He'd had every right to do so—a fact that made her wonder if she was taking advantage of his good graces.

He ended the call less than a minute later. "She's on it. She's calling the bank and is going to start the warrant process right away. I think it might be a good idea if we just swing by the local branch on the way back to the precinct. What do you say? I know your privileges have been somewhat revoked, but you still know how to flash that ID, right?"

"I do." And it wasn't like it would be the first time she'd used it when she wasn't supposed to. She'd done it a handful of times since picking her career back up post-retirement.

He continued to search around her browsing history but the only other comment he made between their and the local banking branch Jennifer used was: "Damn, this woman loves Pinterest."

"You know the NYPD better than I do," Kate said. "How long on that warrant?"

"With the FBI pushing for it, I'd guess two or three hours."

"Not bad. I wonder if there's anything we can do at the station until it comes through."

"There's always digging through research," Pritchard joked.

But that was perfectly fine with Kate. In fact, *anything* she could do to help in that moment would be welcome.

***

When Kate parked in the bank lot, she felt the pressure of the day on her. She could almost hear the ticking of a clock, counting down not only the moments until Jennifer Nobilini would be released, but the moments until her likely removal from the bureau and any legal damages that might come about as a result of Jennifer's hasty and public arrest.

When they walked into the bank, Kate carried the warrant with her. It had taken two hours and twenty minutes to get it in her hands—nothing short of a miracle based on some of the experiences Kate had seen in the past.

They discreetly share their business with a woman at the front cashier's window and were then asked to wait one moment. It was a quick moment, no more than twenty seconds, before they were greeted by an older man who came from somewhere in the back of the bank.

"Are you the agents asking about a client's accounts?" the man asked. His name tag identified him as Ray Kirby.

"Yes," Kate said, showing her ID and cringing internally as she did so. "I'm Agent Kate Wise and this is my local assist, Detective Pritchard. We were told Agent DeMarco called ahead for us."

"She did. Come on into my office and let me see what I can do to help you."

He walked quickly, whether out of the excitement of a break in his daily monotony or out of the desire to get a federal agent out of his bank right away, Kate wasn't sure. He led them down a small hallway behind the primary cashier windows and into a large office. He invited them to have a seat in the chairs on the front end of his desk while he sat down behind it.

"I already took the liberty of pulling up Mrs. Nobilini's account information based on what Agent DeMarco told me," he said.

He turned his desktop monitor at an angle where all three of them could see it. "As you can see, most of her transactions are rather large, though there aren't many. But we've tracked this one transaction you see over and over again, and it is to pay off her credit card every month. It seems she puts all expenditures on the cards and pays it off regularly. What I have here on the screen goes back eighteen months and the largest is for a little over three thousand dollars. However, there *is* one large transaction right here," he said, pointing to a transaction from two days before Jack Tucker's death. "And I can't make heads nor tails of where this money was sent. A private account, perhaps."

Kate looked at the transaction. It was a transfer of twenty thousand dollars. Then, below that, there was another transaction, a transfer to the same sender, this one for two thousand dollars.

"What would we need to find out where those transfers were sent?" Kate asked.

"We can try it from here, but it might take a while," Kirby said.

Kate had known this would be the answer; she hated the fact that she knew it would take only a single call to the bureau to get

147

someone started on figuring this out. It might take a day or two to get it cracked, but it would get done. It was just another task she'd have to ask DeMarco to handle, in light of her new designation.

She then looked to Pritchard as one of the strands of her theory started to thrum. "Do you still have Beringer's laptop in your possession?"

"It's stored away in Evidence at the precinct."

And as he said it, he seemed to pick up on her train of thought. He stood up quickly, thanked Ray Kirby for his time, and then hurried out. Kate did the same, loving the thrill of the hunt but wishing she had more time.

***

Within an hour, Kate was back at the precinct, in a conference room with Pritchard, DeMarco, and a few cops who had been assigned to help as needed. Pritchard was working closely with the precinct's top tech guy to figure out where the twenty-thousand-dollar transfer was sent while Kate looked over a printout of all of Jennifer Nobilini's transactions dating all the way back to the year Frank had been killed. It had been waiting for them when they arrived at the station, sent on behalf of Ray Kirby from the bank.

Meanwhile, Jennifer Nobilini's lawyer had showed up. She was practically demanding to speak with Kate, but Kate ignored her. She even had DeMarco threaten to press charges against her if she continued to be so domineering and trying to interrupt the investigation. Kate could actually hear them speaking loudly outside the conference room door as Pritchard knocked on the table's surface in celebration of a discovery.

"We did find something else," he said. "Not where all of that money went, but a Wikihow page. She was looking into how to purchase a large amount of Bitcoin between the time she posted that ad and Jack Tucker was killed. It looks like it might have actually been the same day that Zeus Beringer showed up at Ashton Elementary."

"I know what Bitcoin is but I'm not as cool as I look," Kate said. "Can you explain the relevance?"

"Bitcoin is the basic preferred currency on the dark web. Drugs, prostitution, child pornography, weapons, all of it. About eighty percent of all transactions on the dark web are conducted in Bitcoin."

"Is that what she spent the twenty thousand on?"

"I don't think so. Not unless she was buying them from someone that really went all out on being private. But based on the fact that she wasn't even smart enough to erase her browsing history, I highly doubt it. No...if this money was sent to someone, I think it was a wire transfer and nothing more. But whoever she sent it to directed it to an account that is incredibly difficult to trace. Maybe on offshore account or some sort of encrypted cash-related site on the dark web."

It wasn't the information they were looking for, but it spurred Kate on. They were defiantly on to something...now it just came down to making all of the pieces fit and finding that one last piece that would make it all make sense.

A few moments later, Kate heard a little murmur of excitement from Pritchard and the tech guy as they apparently figured out how to access her history beyond the point of the last time she had cleaned it out.

"Here's something else," Pritchard said. "A little over a month ago, she visited a site that offers dark web software. It spends most of the time describing Tor. But we've already checked her computer for things like that and there's nothing. Maybe she read up on it and got scared."

"Which begs the question why someone like Jennifer Nobilini would even want to access the dark web," Kate said. "Or want any sort of anonymous browsing."

She turned back to the printouts of Jennifer's bank history. She had made her way down to the year of Frank's death. It was the last page of fifteen and it was there that a large number jumped up, springing out of nowhere.

"This might be it," Kate said, pointing to the entry. "Pritchard, look at this. March, eight years ago—a month before Frank was killed. There are three transfers, to an undisclosed recipient."

They all looked to the entries in question: three transfers of twelve thousand dollars, all within a span of four days.

"How did her husband not figure this out?" the tech guy said.

"Because it's a personal account," Kate said. "They might have seemed like a perfect couple to everyone else, but they apparently didn't trust one another with their money."

"So," Pritchard said, "a few days before Frank Nobilini is killed, there are these three transfers from her bank account. Fast forward eight years and there's a twenty-thousand-dollar one and a smaller one to go along with it, just a few days before Jack Tucker is killed. That's not just coincidence."

A knock on the door interrupted them as DeMarco stepped in. "Kate, this lawyer is going to end up pissing me off. Can you just talk to her? Just to shut her up, if nothing else."

"Not yet," Kate said. "DeMarco...look at this. I think we've got her."

DeMarco stepped inside and took a seat at the table. Kate and Pritchard filled her in on the discoveries they'd made since confiscating Jennifer's laptop from the school. A look of something close to fascination came over DeMarco's face as she leaned back in her chair and let out a deep breath.

"That's one hundred percent better than anything I've gotten out of her all morning. She *has* admitted to the affair. But she won't give a name. But with all of this," she said, indicating the laptop and the bank printouts, "the affair seems like small potatoes."

"I want to speak to her," Kate said. "Would you risk calling Duran for me?"

DeMarco hesitated for a moment and then nodded. "Sure," she finally said. "It's not like *my* head is on the line." She then looked to Pritchard and the officer apologetically. "Can we have the room, guys?"

The men nodded and got up without any argument. Pritchard gave Kate a little smile as he walked through the doorway and closed the door behind him.

"This makes no sense to me," DeMarco said. "Sure, I can see where all of these revelations lead, but it makes no sense."

"Not at first," Kate said. "But there's something there, buried under it all." She then took a few seconds to explain her theory to DeMarco—how they had all of the answers and, more importantly, the right person in custody.

DeMarco rubbed at her head in frustration and then pulled out her cell phone. She called Duran, looking back and forth between Kate and the bank printouts. Kate listened as DeMarco filled him in on these new discoveries. She also detected the waver in DeMarco's voice as the conversation reached its end.

"All of this came from Agent Wise," DeMarco said. "And with all due respect, sir, I think she was right earlier. I think the heat between her and Jennifer can work in our favor—especially in light of these new discoveries."

There were a few seconds where Kate could only hear the murmurs of Duran's voice. DeMarco then slowly handed the phone to Kate with a mock look of fright. "He wants to speak to you," she said.

Kate took the phone. She knew that if there was any chance of redeeming herself and potentially salvaging her reputation with the bureau, it rested on this call and anything that came after it.

"Yes, sir?"

"I'll give you fifteen minutes to speak with her," Duran said, short and straight to the point. "If noting comes of it, I want you out of New York right away. If I have to, I'll immediately fire you and have you escorted out of the city by the police. Please don't make me do that, Kate."

"I won't. Thank you, sir."

She ended the call and handed the phone back to DeMarco. An uncomfortable silence hung between them for a moment before DeMarco broke it. "Be careful," she said. "I honestly hate you a little bit for stealing the show from me, but that doesn't mean I want you to go in there and totally ruin your second career run."

Kate smiled. *Second career run. Is that what this is?*

"Thanks, DeMarco. You want to come in with me?"

"No. I'm good watching from the observation room." She opened the door for Kate and said: "Good work. I...well, I never get tired of being surprised by you."

"I could say the same for you."

DeMarco smiled and headed out. "Let me make it easier for you. Give me two minutes and I'll have a few of the policemen take the lawyer in another room, pretending to care about what Jennifer is claiming as her side of the story."

"Duran would not approve of that," Kate pointed out with her own smile.

DeMarco only shrugged as she started down the hall.

And with that, Kate left the conference room and headed down the hall to speak with Jennifer Nobilini one last time.

CHAPTER TWENTY EIGHT

When Kate was sure that DeMarco had occupied the lawyer with a few poor policemen, she entered the interrogation room. Jennifer sat up straight in her chair behind the basic interrogation table. She looked like a tiger had entered the room, not a fifty-six-year-old woman. She looked beyond Kate, to the door as it closed, as if hoping someone else would be entering as well.

"What the hell are *you* doing here?" Jennifer asked.

"I don't like leaving loose ends untied. Also, I thought I'd give you a proper thank-you for filing that complaint to my boss. That made my day a lot more pleasant."

"Did you think I was bluffing?" Jennifer asked.

Kate sat down in the other chair across the table from Jennifer. "Oh, no. I'm beginning to understand that you aren't the sort of woman that bluffs. You pretty much shoot straight from the hip, don't you?"

"So why are you here, Agent Wise? Trying to dig up more dirt? Want to try to pin something else on me in addition to adultery?"

Kate smiled, a little amused at how easily this evil woman was falling right into her hands. "As a matter of fact, yes. You see...I know you think that you're very smart and very clever. And for all I know, that is true for certain things. But not when it comes to covering your ass." She gave Jennifer a moment to respond but when it was clear that she was going to remain quiet, she added: "When the fire alarm sounded this morning, you left your computer in the gym. It was unlocked and I got to it before the password screen could come up. For a woman trying to hide things from people, you should know to delete your browsing history more often."

True fear shone in Jennifer's eyes for the first time but she did her best to hide it. She sat up as rigid as a slab of stone and said, "I won't say another word without my lawyer."

Kate smiled again and leaned in close. "Are you sure about that? Because your browsing history is not the worst of your problems. If you really want your lawyer here, that's fine. But it might serve your pretty little reputation a bit better if she *doesn't* hear what I'm about to say over the next few minutes. Your call."

Jennifer sneered at her with such force that Kate would not have been surprised if the woman were to spit in her face. "Say what you need to say then."

"I'll say this: I find it very odd indeed that there are significant bank transfers from your account to some undisclosed and secretive recipient within several days of not only your own husband's death, but Jack Tucker's as well. I also find it a little peculiar that you took the time to look into how to make sure you didn't get caught—looking into dark web software and using bitcoins for your transactions—but decided against it. Why was that, Jennifer? Would doing such things make you feel as if you were actually *guilty*?"

"This is ridiculous," she said. "I did not kill my husband! And I didn't even know Jack Tucker!"

"Oh, I'm not accusing you of killing your husband. I don't think you have it in you."

"Then why are you bringing it up?"

"Well…it all comes down to a man named Zeus Beringer. Did you know him?"

She hesitated, clearly acting—and doing a decent job of it. "No. Should I?"

"Well, we're fairly certain he killed Jack Tucker. It's hard to tell, though. We can't question him because he's dead. Recently dead."

"What does he have to do with this?"

"You know him," Kate said. "Maybe very well."

"No. I told you…I don't know that name."

Ignoring her, Kate went on with her interrogation technique. "Well, maybe you didn't know him all that well. You don't have to know someone very well to kill them, do you?"

"You're insane!"

"Four times. With his own gun. The same gun that killed Jack Tucker…and Frank all those years ago."

That's what did it. She tried to hide the reaction of hearing the connection, of hearing her sins so blatantly in her face. The question roaring through her head might as well have been written on her forehead in bright red marker: *How do you know that?*

"Here are the facts of the case, Mrs. Nobilini," Kate said, knowing she had her now. "Stop me when you hear something that isn't correct. Your husband and Jack Tucker were both killed by the same type of weapon within just a few days of large transactions being made in your bank account. This time around, the transactions did not total quite as much—and perhaps *because* of that, the man you hired was not pleased. Maybe he wanted more money. Maybe you were going outside of whatever terms you two had agreed to. So to make sure you paid what he wanted, he put a scare in you by showing up at your kids' school. Does that sound about right?"

Jennifer said nothing but her tears and trembling gave the answer.

"I suppose this motivated you to do what you could, to maybe call him off. So you met with him. Maybe then you—"

"It was my children," Jennifer said, softly.

"I'm sorry, can you repeat that?"

"My children! He was after my children and...and I knew that I was over my head. He had come for my children."

"Do you want to tell me why he was a piece of this at all? Eight years after you hired him to kill your husband? Why again?"

"Because..."

It was a word that was just as good as an admission. She *had* hired Zeus to kill her husband eight years ago. She was not doing anything to argue against it.

"Jennifer?"

"Because I saw it in Missy, too! On two different occasions, I heard her gripe about her husband, how he was boring her to death, how she wanted out of her life. She'd had an affair and felt guilt-ridden over it. And I...I felt sorry for her! I had been there! But I knew how to fix it and..."

"Did she ever ask you to?" Kate asked.

"No. But she said she was going to tell her husband. She said she had to. Said the guilt was too much. To love another man while her boring, useless husband was not paying her the attention she deserved..."

"So you spent at least twenty thousand dollars to release another woman from her marriage? Is that about right?"

Jennifer slammed her fists down on the table and when she looked at Kate, Kate saw something in her eyes that was more than fury or sadness. There was something there that seemed unhinged—something she had seen sparks of in the eyes of men and women who had worked toward an insanity plea and, more often than not, got it. It wasn't a complete surprise to Kate; she'd glimpsed the slightest bit of it when she had confronted her about her affair the first time.

"Yes!" She then let out a roar of a scream that turned into an obscenity. "She was so fucking weak! She would have told her husband and he would have left her and taken the kids. Her life

154

would have been over! She would have never gotten to see her kids and she'd have a reputation…would probably never find anyone else. She would been ruined. So I freed her of it…"

"So you were friends? Close friends?"

"Of course, you moron! Why the hell else would I do it? I told her about two mornings ago. I told her what I had done, to free her. She…she snapped on me. But she also wanted to protect me. So we pretended we didn't know each other well. Great FBI work on your part there, I have to say."

Kate let the comment slide off her back, recalling how she'd thought Missy had been lying about whether she had told anyone other than Jasmine Brooks about her affair. *She'd told Jennifer, too,* Kate thought. *Maybe more than she told Jasmine.*

"You hired him for the murder of Jack Tucker," Kate said. "There was a discrepancy of some kind, he went after your kids, and you killed him. You arranged a meeting with him at the Comfort Inn in the Bronx and you killed him."

"With his own gun, too," she said, rather proudly. "He thought I was going to sleep with him to buy me some time for the rest of the payment. And just as things got heated, I kicked him in the balls, grabbed his gun—I guess he never goes anywhere without it or he was thinking I was going to turn him in or something. And then I k…I killed him."

The last three words caused her to weep. Saying it out loud apparently brought it home for her. With her money, she had killed two men. But she had killed Zeus Beringer with her own hands, by her own plans and action.

Kate slowly got up and headed for the door. She damn near felt sorry for Jennifer Nobilini. The woman was clearly unhinged but the question that remained was whether she had always been this way or if it had happened after she had arranged for her husband to be killed eight years ago.

"You understand, right?" Jennifer screamed as Kate reached for the door. "Missy Tucker was weak and was going to waste her life with a man that did not deserve her. I was helping. I was freeing her."

"Why don't you ask her how being a widow feels right now?" Kate asked, a tremor in her own voice "Why don't you ask her children how they feel to not have a father?"

"And what about mine?" Jennifer hissed. "I'll go to prison for this. They'll not have a mother…no one to look after them."

"That's right," Kate said. "It's a damn shame you also made sure they don't have a father."

155

Kate opened the door and closes it quickly to shut out Jennifer's wails of sorrow and anger. Kate realized that she was also weeping and quickly wiped a tear away before anyone could see it.

DeMarco came out of the observation room, a look of respect and shock in her eyes. "Jesus, Kate...that was brutal. And it took less than ten minutes." She tapped her pocket, making a knocking noise against her phone. "Also, Duran called me back immediately after you went in there. Said he wanted to see it. So I FaceTimed him. He saw the whole thing. I think it's safe to say your job is safe. That was...that was impressive."

"I don't know about the job part of it," she said. "But thanks for the compliment. I feel sort of like a bitch for how I just wrecked that poor woman. But hiring someone to kill a husband...it..."

She had to stop here as visions of Michael and his smiling face came flooding into her head.

"Kate?"

"Sorry...I just need a minute."

She rushed away from DeMarco, in search of the nearest restroom. And as she went looking, she could still hear Jennifer Nobilini's cries as her lawyer finally entered the room.

CHAPTER TWENTY NINE

Kate woke up three days later to someone knocking on her front door. She sat up in bed and looked at the clock. When she saw that it was eight in the morning and realized that she had slept for almost nine hours, she felt instantly energized even though her eyes were still heavy with sleep. She got out of bed, shoved her feet into her slippers, and walked through her house to the front door.

When she opened it and saw Allen on the other side, she was shocked. She had no idea what to say, no idea how to react. They had not spoken since he had told her on the phone that he wasn't sure he was a good fit for her chaotic life. But now here he was standing on her front porch carrying a box of bagels and a drink coaster with two coffees from her favorite coffee shop just down the street.

"I figured if I showed up with coffee, you might let me come in," he said.

"You were right," Kate said, plucking one of the coffees out of the carrier. She let him inside and then closed the door behind her. They walked into the kitchen without talking and settled down at the table.

"I usually don't question handsome men that bring me coffee," Kate said, "but what are you doing here?"

He sighed and picked a bagel from the box. As he opened up a carry-out container of hazelnut cream cheese, she could tell that he was nervous.

"I hope you don't mind, but I texted Melissa yesterday. I wanted to know if you were done with this latest case you were on and if you were back home yet. And based on the last conversation we had, I didn't think you'd want me calling or texting you."

"It would have been okay."

"Well, I wasn't sure. Anyway, Melissa didn't text me back. She called me. And she and I had a very good conversation."

"Dare I ask what about?"

He had layered his bagel with cream cheese and now took a bite. He answered as he chewed—a pet peeve of Kate's but he somehow managed to make it cute.

"She called me to ask if I thought she was being selfish because she doesn't like you going back to work. She told me her worries and about the conversations you two have had about it. I told her I thought it was a perfectly normal reaction but that I wasn't the best person to ask about it. I told her about our phone conversation—about me trying to break things off—and she proceeded to tell me I was an idiot."

"Yeah, that sounds like Melissa."

"Your daughter…she's very much like you. She let me know that you were always like this with your job and that it's not because you don't care about family and friends but because you're so passionate about your job—about helping other people."

"She didn't see it that way when she was younger."

"I know. She told me all about that."

"Is there anything you *didn't* talk about?"

"No. We covered everything. We're, like, besties now."

"Please, Allen. Never say *besties* again. Ever."

He nodded and sipped from his coffee. "But you know, I think she's right. I've seen it in you all over the place—the way you care about people. The way you love your job, your daughter and your granddaughter. In the way you tip *way* too much at restaurants. And I started to think about how someone with that kind of a heart must be affected by a job like yours. A job you returned to after retirement because you cared so much about it."

"Allen, but you were right. I did put my job above others sometimes. I don't mean to, but it does happen from time to time. Melissa suffered from it when she was younger. And Michael…there are so many things I wished we could have done differently. Spent more time together…but I can't now. And my job is to blame for that."

"I won't presume to know how your late husband felt about such things," Allen said. "But if he passed on any of his traits to Melissa, I can pretty much guarantee you that he understood it."

"I don't know how much longer I can do it anyway," Kate said. "If at all. This last case…it just proved that at my age, I tend to get to personally connected. To the case, to the people I meet, to DeMarco…"

"And that's a bad thing?" Allen asked.

"My director thinks so. And with good cause."

She thought about the last conversation she'd had with DeMarco, during the debrief on the afternoon of Jennifer Nobilini's arrest. She'd commended her for her work but they had left the meeting with her future very much up in the air. And the only thing that had eased that awkwardness was a visit to Cass Nobilini to let her know that her son's killer had been found and brought to justice.

She had left the finer details out, stating that it had been the work of Zeus Beringer. It was not the entire truth, but it had been enough for a mother who could finally find that sense of closure that had eluded her for so long.

"Well, I'd like to ask that you forget everything I said on the phone," Allen said, bringing her back into the present. "I was irritated and lonely and...worried about you. Just like your daughter. We both love you and—"

He realized what he had said and stopped himself with another mouthful of bagel.

"Don't dodge it," Kate said with a smile. "I heard it. You said it."

"Shit. I guess I did. But it's true. I worry about you because I love you. I have for a few weeks now, I think. And I think that's where my pushing came from. So please...can we pretend it never happened?"

"Only if you tell me everything you and Melissa talked about."

"Sorry," he said. "Can't. Besties don't share each other's secrets."

Kate laughed and tossed her bagel at him. He dodged it, reached out and took her hand, and pulled her forward. When he kissed her, Kate thought that it felt right—more right than it ever had before.

She supposed she loved him, too. And that was a hard thing for her to admit. Not just because of Michael and her job but because she knew that when she loved, she loved hard. She wasn't sure if she would be capable of such a thing this late in her life.

Are you really going to deny yourself the chance, though? she asked herself.

It was a good question, especially coming off of a case where she had spent most of the time dwelling in the past. When she looked beyond that case, beyond the Nobilinis and the Tuckers, there was more past there—a past where she had cheated her family of memories and affection because of her job.

If she had learned anything from solving those two murders, it was that the past was always there, always offering memories and lessons that she could use to learn from and to fix present-day hurts.

And as their kiss deepened, she thought it would certainly be worth trying with Allen. And with Melissa and Michelle, and on and on until she could truly leave her past behind her.

IF SHE HID
(A Kate Wise Mystery—Book 4)

"A masterpiece of thriller and mystery. Blake Pierce did a magnificent job developing characters with a psychological side so well described that we feel inside their minds, follow their fears and cheer for their success. Full of twists, this book will keep you awake until the turn of the last page."
--Books and Movie Reviews, Roberto Mattos (re Once Gone)

IF SHE HID (A Kate Wise Mystery) is book #4 in a new psychological thriller series by bestselling author Blake Pierce, whose #1 bestseller Once Gone (Book #1) (a free download) has received over 1,000 five star reviews.

Two parents are found dead, and their twin 16 year old daughters are missing. With the case quickly growing cold, the FBI, stumped, must summon their most brilliant agent: retired 55 year old FBI agent Kate Wise.

Was this a random murder? The work of a serial killer?

Can they find the girls in time?

And does Kate, haunted by her past, still have the ability to solve cases as she used to?

An action-packed thriller with heart-pounding suspense, IF SHE HID is book #4 in a riveting new series that will leave you turning pages late into the night.

Book #5 in the KATE WISE MYSTERY SERIES will be available soon.

Blake Pierce

Blake Pierce is author of the bestselling RILEY PAGE mystery series, which includes fifteen books (and counting). Blake Pierce is also the author of the MACKENZIE WHITE mystery series, comprising nine books (and counting); of the AVERY BLACK mystery series, comprising six books; of the KERI LOCKE mystery series, comprising five books; of the MAKING OF RILEY PAIGE mystery series, comprising three books (and counting); of the KATE WISE mystery series, comprising four books (and counting); of the CHLOE FINE psychological suspense mystery, comprising three books (and counting); and of the JESSE HUNT psychological suspense thriller series, comprising three books (and counting).

An avid reader and lifelong fan of the mystery and thriller genres, Blake loves to hear from you, so please feel free to visit www.blakepierceauthor.com to learn more and stay in touch.

BOOKS BY BLAKE PIERCE

A JESSIE HUNT PSYCHOLOGICAL SUSPENSE SERIES
THE PERFECT WIFE (Book #1)
THE PERFECT BLOCK (Book #2)
THE PERFECT HOUSE (Book #3)

CHLOE FINE PSYCHOLOGICAL SUSPENSE SERIES
NEXT DOOR (Book #1)
A NEIGHBOR'S LIE (Book #2)
CUL DE SAC (Book #3)

KATE WISE MYSTERY SERIES
IF SHE KNEW (Book #1)
IF SHE SAW (Book #2)
IF SHE RAN (Book #3)
IF SHE HID (Book #4)

THE MAKING OF RILEY PAIGE SERIES
WATCHING (Book #1)
WAITING (Book #2)
LURING (Book #3)

RILEY PAIGE MYSTERY SERIES
ONCE GONE (Book #1)
ONCE TAKEN (Book #2)
ONCE CRAVED (Book #3)
ONCE LURED (Book #4)
ONCE HUNTED (Book #5)
ONCE PINED (Book #6)
ONCE FORSAKEN (Book #7)
ONCE COLD (Book #8)
ONCE STALKED (Book #9)
ONCE LOST (Book #10)
ONCE BURIED (Book #11)
ONCE BOUND (Book #12)
ONCE TRAPPED (Book #13)
ONCE DORMANT (book #14)
ONCE SHUNNED (Book #15)

MACKENZIE WHITE MYSTERY SERIES
BEFORE HE KILLS (Book #1)

BEFORE HE SEES (Book #2)
BEFORE HE COVETS (Book #3)
BEFORE HE TAKES (Book #4)
BEFORE HE NEEDS (Book #5)
BEFORE HE FEELS (Book #6)
BEFORE HE SINS (Book #7)
BEFORE HE HUNTS (Book #8)
BEFORE HE PREYS (Book #9)
BEFORE HE LONGS (Book #10)
BEFORE HE LAPSES (Book #11)

AVERY BLACK MYSTERY SERIES
CAUSE TO KILL (Book #1)
CAUSE TO RUN (Book #2)
CAUSE TO HIDE (Book #3)
CAUSE TO FEAR (Book #4)
CAUSE TO SAVE (Book #5)
CAUSE TO DREAD (Book #6)

KERI LOCKE MYSTERY SERIES
A TRACE OF DEATH (Book #1)
A TRACE OF MUDER (Book #2)
A TRACE OF VICE (Book #3)
A TRACE OF CRIME (Book #4)
A TRACE OF HOPE (Book #5)